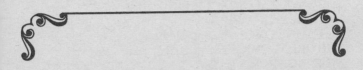
Lydia resumed what she considered the walk of a lightskirt.

"Better," he murmured. "But your superior bit o' muslin don't wiggle. She sways."

She felt his hand on her hip, not lightly, but holding firmly.

"There, that is much better," he said in a voice suddenly husky. Lydia removed his hand and pinched it as hard as she could.

"Temper, temper, my pet. You are doing just fine for a tyro." His dark eyes gazed into hers, which were sparkling with annoyance and something else—amusement, was it? For a long moment they simply stared at each other; then his head inclined slowly to hers. . . .

By Joan Smith
Published by Fawcett Books:

THE SAVAGE LORD GRIFFIN
GATHER YE ROSEBUDS
AUTUMN LOVES: An Anthology
THE GREAT CHRISTMAS BALL
NO PLACE FOR A LADY
NEVER LET ME GO
REGENCY MASQUERADE
THE KISSING BOUGH
A REGENCY CHRISTMAS: An Anthology
DAMSEL IN DISTRESS
BEHOLD, A MYSTERY!
A KISS IN THE DARK
THE VIRGIN AND THE UNICORN
A TALL DARK STRANGER
TEA AND SCANDAL
A CHRISTMAS GAMBOL
AN INFAMOUS PROPOSAL
PETTICOAT REBELLION
BLOSSOM TIME
MURDER WILL SPEAK
MURDER AND MISDEEDS
MURDER WHILE I SMILE
MURDER COMES TO MIND
A HIGHWAYMAN CAME RIDING
LITTLE COQUETTE

LITTLE COQUETTE

Joan Smith

FAWCETT CREST • NEW YORK

A Fawcett Crest Book
Published by The Ballantine Publishing Group
Copyright © 1998 by Joan Smith

http://www.randomhouse.com

Library of Congress Catalog Card Number: 97-94532

ISBN 0-449-00153-9

Manufactured in the United States of America

First Edition: July 1998

10 9 8 7 6 5 4 3 2 1

LITTLE COQUETTE

Chapter One

"I wonder how poor Horace Findley is bearing up since his Alice died," Lady Trevelyn said, peering at the embroidery pattern recently purchased from Mr. Wilks of Regent Street. She was a devotee of the new fad for Berlin wool-work. The project on which she was presently embarked was a canvas to be framed and hung in Sir John's study. It depicted a scene from Walter Scott's *Guy Mannering.* In it, young Harry Bertram had been kidnapped and carried to Holland, which allowed the picture to include masses of tulips and a windmill. So pleased was Lady Trevelyn with her execution of the flowers that she was inclined to omit Harry from the scene.

"Such good neighbors the Findleys have always been. I ought to visit Horace more often," she said, "but then one would not want to cause talk, calling too frequently on a widower."

It would take an active imagination to cast Lady Trevelyn in the role of seductress. Her once pretty face was set in the rigid lines of propriety. The steel gray curls peering out from the edge of her cap might have been fashioned by a blacksmith. Her spreading girth was tightly compacted into a gown of puce lutestring, which was her notion of gaiety to welcome spring. In winter she wore black.

1

"Mr. Findley seems to be bearing up well," her daughter replied. Lydia Trevelyn's appearance was strikingly different from her mama's. The classical lineaments of her face, her intelligent gray eyes and black hair, even her willowy frame were all inherited from her papa's side of the family. At eighteen years she was in her prime. The flaw that marred an otherwise unexceptionable young lady was a tendency to willfulness.

She did not indulge in embroidery, watercolors, flower arranging, or any of the customary feminine pastimes. Papa's sister, her aunt Nessie, had given her a copy of Mary Wollstonecraft's *Vindication of the Rights of Woman* for Christmas. Lydia had read it with a sense of revelation. At the beginning of the new year, she had exchanged her needle for a cudgel. She now had confirmation of what she always suspected, that ladies' inferior position in society was due to their lack of education, and she determined on the spot to improve her mind. It was not to the classics of the Greeks and Romans that she applied herself, but to the daily journals. Her father, Sir John, had inculcated the notion that his own sphere, politics, was what made the world go round.

She pored over incomprehensible political articles, hoping that one day they would become clear to her. As her papa was now at home suffering from gout, she took every opportunity to quiz him. She was beginning to get a grasp on the Corn Laws. Her next object was the Holy Alliance, which appeared to have more to do with politics than religion.

"A pity Horace has no son," Lady Trevelyn continued. "I am happy to say I gave your papa a son,

2

Lydia. It is a wife's duty in marriage to give her husband a son and heir."

"Yes indeed! It would be a great pity if a daughter were to inherit anything," Lydia replied.

Her mama heard the words but failed to recognize the sarcasm. "A tragedy," she said. "Mind you, daughters have their place. How else is the world to go on if gentlemen have no one to marry? If a young lady has the good fortune to marry a fortune and title, then a son is her foremost, one might almost say her only, concern."

"Like a brood mare," Lydia murmured.

"No need to bring the barnyard into a polite saloon, my dear. We are speaking of ladies and gentlemen—and marriage."

The sharp look that accompanied this speech was a tacit reminder of the excellent title and fortune up for grabs at the neighboring estate, Pontneuf Chase, where the dashing Marquess of Beaumont had yet to bestow his title and worldly goods on a damsel. Who more fitting than his neighbor? And really, how else was Lydia to be bounced off, when she refused to be presented in London as she ought? As to calling the Marriage Mart a human cattle auction! It was too bad of Sir John to let Lydia wrap him around her finger. He had acquiesced so easily, one would almost think he did not want Lydia and herself in London.

That Lady Trevelyn did not want to endure the commotion of a Season was beside the point. She would have gone if Sir John had insisted. Of course, Nessie could have handled all the details of the presentation. She was good at that sort of thing, whereas Lady Trevelyn would have been out of her depth. After having presented her huband with the

3

requisite son and a daughter, she had retired to Trevelyn Hall while Sir John spent most of the year in London, where he was a distinguished member of the Tory government. The arrangement suited them both down to the heels.

"I must see to your papa's posset," she said, setting aside her canvas and woolen threads with a sigh. "He is suffering so with his gout. You know how he hates to miss a day in the House. He is like a bear after losing a whole week. I hope he is well enough to return soon. Why don't you go out for a walk, Lydia? You are looking peaky. It is what comes of living with your nose stuck in a journal. Ladies have no need to read such heavy stuff. It brings on wrinkles." She scanned her daughter's face for signs of this tragedy.

Lydia had no objection to escaping into the sunshine of a warm spring morning. She decided to take her fishing rod down to the river that formed a border between Trevelyn Hall and Pontneuf Chase and try to catch that big trout that had eluded her papa for five years now, and herself for the two months since she had decided she would fish, since it was frowned upon for ladies. As her mama would either rant or cry at such unladylike doings, Lydia took the precaution of leaving her rod in the gardener's shed. Martin, the head gardener, would attach the bait for her. That was one masculine perquisite she was not eager to assume.

"After Old Finny again, are you, Miss Lydia?" he asked, handing her the rod. He ought to have called her Miss Trevelyn, but Lydia's quest for fair treatment extended beyond ladies to include all the oppressed. If a faithful old retainer wished to call her Miss Lydia, who was she to object?

4

"I'll catch the rascal yet, Martin," she replied, watching as he attached a fly to the hook.

"Mind you don't scratch yourself," he cautioned, and wrapped a leaf around the baited hook to prevent an accident.

Lydia usually resented being spoken to as if she were a child or an idiot, but she accepted Martin's admonition without comment, as she knew he meant well. She tipped the rod over her shoulder and scampered down the grassy slope to the river. Pontneuf River was more like an overgrown stream than a river. It had a pretty humpbacked bridge that joined Lord Beaumont's acres to her papa's. It was from the bridge that she usually fished. She removed the leaf from the hook, cast her line into the water, and began to reel it in.

She didn't really like fishing, especially when she accidentally caught a slimy old fish with its mouth open. In fact, she did not much enjoy reading the hard news either. At such moments of quiet reflection as this, at peace with nature, she had an unsettling notion that gentlemen's lives were not all they were cracked up to be. Her own papa worked so very hard, he was hardly ever home. As the sun glinted over the surface of the stream, she reviewed for perhaps the hundredth time what was to become of her. She would not inherit Trevelyn Hall. That would go to her brother, Tom, after Papa's death. Tom was attending university. He had been invited to spend a holiday with a fellow student in Devonshire. Lord Henry Haversham had two well-dowered sisters, which was why Mama had not only allowed the visit but encouraged it.

Lydia would inherit her mama's ten thousand dowry. Ten thousand, while it might buy a respectable husband, was hardly enough for her to live on her own in the style she was accustomed to. Yet she would not consider living at the Hall after Tom married, under his thumb—and his wife's.

She wanted to engage in some meaningful work in any case, not fritter her life away, but the careers open to ladies were so few and so demeaning and so poorly paid that she had no taste for them. In her youthful idealism, she envisaged herself a famous philanthropist, helping the needy. Wrapped up in her dreams, she did not see the gentleman hastening down the bank on the other side of the river.

Lord Beaumont saw her, however, and was careful to avoid the bridge where Lydia stood. It annoyed him that a female had invaded this masculine preserve. It was his favorite spot for being alone. Sometimes he indulged in Chinese fishing with no bait on his hook, just sitting, dangling a line in the water, thinking about life. He had taken his seat in the House that spring and was beginning to think seriously about this business of governing the masses.

He threw his curled beaver and blue superfine jacket aside and fished from his own bank, concealed by a thornbush. Hot from the London Season, he was not impressed by Lydia's provincial charms. Her hair was dark and modestly arranged. He preferred a fashionable riot of blond curls. He had never noticed what color her eyes were but he knew she didn't manage them in the artful way the ladies in London did. While she was handsome enough, she was too prudish to suit him. No idea how to flirt. She had snapped his head off at the assembly Saturday evening. She had been complaining of the heat and he suggested in the kindest way possible that she might like to try the dampened gowns that were the latest craze in London.

"You might like to try wearing a wet shirt and see how comfortable it is," she had snapped at him.

He didn't blame Sir John for virtually living apart from his wife. Only thing to do with a harridan like Lady Trevelyn. The on dit in London was that his mistress was a charming redhead.

Beaumont felt a jerk on the end of his line and moved to the bank's edge to reel in his catch. The weight told him he had caught a whopper. His rod bent under the force of it. In his excitement, he cried out, "I've hooked Old Finny!"

Lydia looked up and saw him, straining to reel in the trout. Without thinking, she hooked her own line under a strut of the bridge railing, hiked up her skirt, and ran toward Beaumont. Old Finny was a legend. If Beau had really caught him, it would be as great a marvel as finding the pot of gold at the end of the rainbow or winning the state lottery. As she ran toward him, she noticed the rod was not jumping as it would if he had a large fish on the end of his line. There was tension on it all right, but it was a deadweight.

"You've got your hook caught on a sunken log," she said, in that condescending manner that set his teeth on edge.

By this time, Beaumont realized his catch was not putting up much of a fight, but he disliked to be told it by a mere chit. He was sorry he'd let her know he was there. "No, it's moving."

"You're going to break your rod. Why don't you cut the line?"

He bit back the childish retort "Why don't you

7

mind your own business?" and said grimly, "It's coming in, whatever it is. Weighs a ton."

"Probably a fallen branch."

"There's a legend of buried treasure in this river. Some ancestor threw a chest of gold coin into the river to hide it from Cromwell's men."

Lydia lifted an eyebrow and said dismissively, "That old chestnut! The water is not deep enough. It's only eighteen inches in late summer."

With the excitement of catching Old Finny dissipating, Lydia just watched Beaumont reel in whatever tree stump or debris he had hooked. Her mama had been puffing this neighbor off as a prime catch since Lydia first let down her skirts, and her aversion to him had grown apace. She suspected that Beaumont's mama held the same cherished dream as her own, which would account for his aversion to her. In the old days, they had been as friendly as the eight-year disparity in their ages allowed.

She acknowledged that he was handsome, rich, and titled. There was no arguing with facts. His six-foot frame was broad shouldered, well muscled, long legged. Sunlight gleamed on bluish black hair so carefully barbered, it sat like a silken cap on his head, with one little lock tumbling over his brow to ruin the elegant effect. A straight nose and rugged jaw lent masculinity to his finely chiseled face. His eyes, she knew, were a deep, inky blue, with long eyelashes like a lady's. She decided it was his looks and eligibility that gave him that overbearing, condescending air that so annoyed her.

"I would cut the line if I were you," she repeated, and turned to leave.

"It's coming—I've got it!" he exclaimed, and began reeling in his line more easily, but the deadweight

8

was still attached, arching the pole until it was in danger of breaking. The muscles of his broad shoulders and strong arms firmed and bulged with the effort.

Lydia watched, unimpressed, and waited, ready to say "I told you so." A sodden jacket was the first thing to surface. It was impossible to tell its original color. It now looked black.

"Someone lost his coat," she said. Before she could have her laugh, a bonnet bobbed up. It had once been an elegant chapeau. Its high poke drooped, but one could still determine its original shape and color. Red—hardly a lady's color. The feathers were waterlogged and bedraggled, which did not conceal either their length or excess of numbers.

"How strange!" she cried, staring at Beaumont as a shiver scuttled up her spine. She was familiar with all the stylish bonnets in the parish. She had never seen this one before. Beaumont was frowning at it and still reeling as hard as he could. The bonnet moved sluggishly, then slowly turned over. Beneath the gliding water, a ghastly white face appeared, with its eyes open and its mouth wide, as if frozen in a cry of anguish.

"Oh my God!" she gasped, and turned as pale as the face in the water. She quickly averted her gaze, then slowly turned back to see if she recognized the woman. She had never seen her before. Beaumont waded into the water up to the edges of his top boots to haul the body out by the shoulders. The head fell back like a rag doll's. He laid the corpse carefully on the grass and arranged the dripping skirts around the black kid slippers.

"Do you know her?" he asked, staring in bewilderment at the awful spectacle on the ground.

9

Lydia was determined not to display any feminine weakness. Beaumont was behaving just as he ought, and she could do no less. She willed down a fit of nausea and forced herself to study the face. In a tightly controlled voice she said, "No, I have never seen her before. She is not from these parts. She hasn't been in the water long. Who could she be?"

"I have no idea."

Water dripped from the woman's eyelashes and rolled down her cheeks, giving a ghoulish semblance of life, as if she were crying. "For goodness' sake, can't you cover her face?" Lydia said.

He drew out his handkerchief and placed it over the woman's face. "I'll stay here. You'd best go for help, Miss Trevelyn. My place is closer."

She took one last look at the covered face and the bonnet, noticing the limp red hair that hung out beneath it in sodden clumps, before running up the hill on trembling legs.

Beaumont remained behind, wondering how a lightskirt had ended up in his river. When Lydia was gone, he lifted the handkerchief and studied the pale face. He didn't recognize this woman, but he knew her calling by her clothes and the faint patches of rouge still visible on her pallid cheeks. Ladies did not wear red bonnets with such a super-fluity of gaudy feathers. They did not wear such low-cut gowns in the daytime, and it was a muslin afternoon frock the woman wore. The bonnet and slippers, all her toilette suggested she was dressed for afternoon. He guessed her age to be in the thirties. Not in the first blush of youth, but not hagged either. Her face was a pretty heart shape with a slightly retroussé nose. She must have been pretty when she was alive. The state of the remains suggested she had not been in the water for more than a day.

How had she come here? At least there was no sign of foul play. She had not been strangled or stabbed or beaten. She could not have come in a carriage or her driver would have reported her missing. The outfit, those kid slippers, said she had not ridden. Had she walked, stopped to look at the river, and slid down the bank? But the water was not deep enough to drown her. It was not over her head. Perhaps she had bumped her head? He hadn't the stomach to remove her bonnet and examine her scalp. Let the sawbones do it. It was odd that her body had been so firmly lodged beneath the water. Almost as if someone had tried to wedge her under a rock or submerged tree.

He looked down at the slippers and noticed the left one was badly scraped, the silk stocking torn. How was it possible, if she had accidentally fallen in? Perhaps she had not died here at all, but her body may have been brought here to conceal it. But why? If he had not happened to catch his hook in her jacket, she might have remained there for weeks or months, even years, until any hope of identifying her was gone.

He was sorry Miss Trevelyn had been exposed to such a horrific discovery. Not that she had seemed very upset. Any normal lady would have pitched herself into his arms, sobbing and swooning, but not that cold wench. "She hasn't been in the water long," she had said, as if it were a dead fish she was looking at and not a woman. Who could she be?

His gaze drifted across the river, to the soaring walls of Trevelyn Hall. Sir John's mistress was said to be a redhead. No, it was impossible. The poor girl was some transient who had met with a mishap. It

11

was ridiculous to think for a minute that this was his neighbor's mistress. What the devil would she be doing here? Although it was odd that Sir John had been home for a week. . . .

Chapter Two

The body found in the river caused a great commotion in the neighborhood. Everybody except Sir John was speaking of it. Lady Trevelyn felt the death might upset him when he was ill and had ordered Lydia and the servants not to mention it. Lydia had been seeking an outlet for her energies and felt she had now found something worthwhile to do. She would drive into Kesterly and see what the constable had discovered. She would then undertake to notify the drowned woman's family in some kind and thoughtful manner. There might be something she could do for them. The woman's toilette had not suggested poverty to be sure, but it was not quite tho toilette of a lady either. A milliner, perhaps, to judge by that gaudy bonnet. She would see that the woman had a proper burial.

This was the sort of good work Lady Trevelyn could approve of, especially when it cast Lydia in Lord Beaumont's path. Naturally he would be taking an interest, as the body had been found in his river. He would see how kind Lydia was, how concerned for the less fortunate.

"I shall go with you, Lydia," she said at once, and called for the carriage to be driven the two miles through pleasantly undulating farmland to Kesterly,

13

the village where they bought life's small necessities. For more important purchases such as bonnets, they went the extra few miles to Watford.

John Groom let the ladies out at the Rose and Crown and stabled the carriage. Lydia did not share her mama's enthusiasm to see Lord Beaumont striding down the High Street toward them. She feared he was bent on the same errand as herself.

To show him she had not got the idea from him, she said at once, "We are just on our way to the constable to find out what we can of that unfortunate woman we found this morning, Beaumont. I want to discover if there is anything we can do for her family."

She was not imagining the look of consternation that seized his handsome face. "Oh, I would not do that if I were you, Miss Trevelyn. I have already been there. The constable has assured me he will notify her family. No doubt they will be taking her home for burial soon."

Her chin lifted instinctively at this blatant example of gentlemen thinking they ruled the world. "I shall speak to him all the same," she said.

Her mama adopted a simpering smile. "I am sure there is no need if Beaumont is handling the matter, dear. So kind of him."

"I should like to go, Mama," Lydia insisted in the steely voice that her mama could see was displeasing Beaumont.

"It is really not necessary," he said firmly.

"There might be something a lady can do that a gentleman cannot," Lydia said. "Who is the woman? What is her name?"

Beaumont saw the mulish set of her chin and realized he had to protect Lady Trevelyn from the

14

truth whatever Lydia said. He was not yet sure what the truth was, but his first idea had taken root and grown.

A pretty redhead found dead in the river adjacent to Sir John's property, Sir John missing from London for a week when he virtually never missed a day in the House, and the woman not only dead, not drowned, but shot. The doctor who had written the death certificate had found a bullet had gone straight through her heart. Beaumont had not spotted the bullet hole in her gown. The water had washed away the blood. No identification had been found on her, but when word of the death got about, the constable had heard a rumor that she had been putting up at the Rose and Crown. Beaumont was on his way there to examine her room in hope of learning her name and where she was from. Once he established her identity, he wanted to get Lydia away from her mama long enough to give her some notion of his fears. As her papa's lightskirt was common knowledge, he assumed Lydia knew about her. If, as he thought, the woman had been Trevelyn's mistress, he would visit Sir John and discuss with him how this awful thing had happened, and how they might protect Sir John and his family—and the Tory party. He did not think for a moment that Sir John had killed her, but he might have an idea who had done it. A jealous lover or husband, perhaps. It would not be unusual for a lightskirt to be mixed up in some dangerous illegal business either. Selling confidential government information was one possibility, blackmail another.

"I don't know her name. I am just on my way into the Rose and Crown now to ask if they know anything of her there," he said. Then he turned a smiling face to Lady Trevelyn. "I am convinced you would not wish to involve yourself in such an unpleasant affair, ma'am. Why do you not let Miss Trevelyn and me make the enquiries while you enjoy a drive or call on a friend. I shall undertake to see that your daughter comes to no harm and deliver her home."

Lady Trevelyn was not likely to object to any scheme that threw Lydia in Beaumont's path. "So very thoughtful. Is that not thoughtful of Beaumont, dear? You two run along and I shall drop in and beg a cup of tea from Mrs. Clarke."

Lydia directed a suspicious glance at Beaumont before accepting the offer. "Thank you, Beaumont," she said. "I shall see you at home, Mama."

"Enjoy yourself," her mama said, as gaily as if it were a social outing.

"What have you learned that you don't want Mama to hear?" Lydia asked as soon as they were alone. "The woman means nothing special to Mama. They were not friends or even acquaintances."

"No, I would hardly call Sir John's bit of muslin a friend of your mama. Not that I am sure, but the coincidence of a redheaded lightskirt turning up dead on his doorstep looks suspicious, you must own."

She stared at him in horror, as if he had struck her. "Papa's bit of muslin!" she gasped. "You're mad. Papa doesn't have a mistress. How dare you say such a thing! That is slander, Beaumont. If you repeat that filthy lie, he'll take you to court."

He blinked in astonishment. "Didn't you know? Why the devil do you think he spends so much time in town?"

"For his work, of course. He is very busy in the House. He is on half a dozen committees."

Beaumont realized his error and wished with all his heart he could unsay the fateful words already spoken. He cleared his throat, blushed, and said, "My mistake, Miss Trevelyn. Sorry. Forget I spoke."

"But where did you hear such a thing?"

He waved his hands as if batting away a gnat. "London is a hotbed of gossip. No doubt it was some other Sir John. Or perhaps it was Lord John. It is a common enough name after all."

Strangely, it was his immediate retraction that half convinced her he was telling the truth. Such an idea had never entered Lydia's head. She knew that plenty of other gentlemen entertained themselves with a mistress, but that her papa, whom she looked up to as a demigod, should sink so low knocked the wind out of her. Then an even worse notion seized her.

"Are you suggesting that Papa killed the woman?" she asked. Her eyes were like wild things, staring at him. "That she came pestering him at home and he drowned her?"

"Of course not. She wasn't drowned anyway. She was shot."

"You think Papa shot her!"

"I don't think anything of the sort!" he replied angrily. "I am not even sure she was his mistress. I heard the woman was putting up at the Rose and Crown. I mean to discover her name and ask Sir John if she was his woman. That's all. It would be a great scandal for the Tory party if it were true."

Scowling like a gargoyle, he took a rough grip on her elbow and led her into the Rose and Crown. Lydia was too shaken to argue. She stood a few feet away while Beaumont spoke to the clerk. As the

17

first shock of his accusation was digested, she began to accept what now seemed almost inevitable. Her papa had a mistress. That was why he had not encouraged her to make her debut last April. He didn't want Mama and her to find out. He had complained of the expense, and Mama had agreed that money was a little tight lately. He was squandering his money on a lightskirt. That was why he spent so much time in London, even in summer when the House was not sitting.

Lydia remembered going into his room only last evening to ask him to explain exactly what function the Chancellor of the Exchequer filled. Her papa had been writing something. She assumed it had to do with government business, and had been a little offended that he pushed the paper under the covers so hastily, as if he could not trust his own daughter. She had seen a corner of violet-colored stationery protruding from under the blanket and wondered at it. It had been a billet-doux from her, his mistress.

But surely his mistress was not that creature in the vulgar red bonnet with all the feathers? Her papa was a gentleman of refined taste. His own toilette was a matter of pride with him. No one for jackets but Weston. His boots must be by Hoby, of St. James's Street, who shod the royal family and the Duke of Wellington, and his curled beavers by Baxter. No, if he had a mistress, it was not that woman found in the river. And even if, in the worst case, Papa had gone mad and taken up with such a creature, he could not have killed her, for he had been in bed with gout. He did have gout, didn't he? It was odd, though, that he would not let Mama ask for Dr. Fraser to attend him as he usually did.

"I know the treatment well enough by now," he had said. "Bed rest will cure me."

But he didn't spend all his time in bed. Late one night when everyone had retired she had heard him coming upstairs and had gone to investigate. He was walking without much limping and without his walking stick. She had taken his arm to help him back to his bedchamber.

"Papa! Surely you have not been downstairs! Why did you not call a servant if you needed something?"

"I mustn't let my legs atrophy," he had said. "Truth to tell, I was after a nip of brandy and didn't want anyone to know. No need to tell your mama. I am feeling a little better this evening."

"Don't get better too quickly, Papa," she had said, tucking him in. "We want you home a little longer." He hadn't been carrying the brandy bottle with him. His breath hadn't smelled of brandy either, had it?

He often stayed in London when he had these attacks of gout. Why had he come home this time? In the first heat of anger, she could believe anything of him. Had he had a falling out with his lover? Had she jilted him, and in an excess of jealousy, had Papa killed her? But he would hardly do it here, on his own doorstep.

The answer came in a blinding flash. Papa had jilted her, and she had come threatening to tell Mama. She was holding him to ransom for some huge sum. That was why money was tight. If Papa had not done the deed himself, he might have hired someone else to do it. Lydia was in a chastened, uncertain state when Beaumont returned, dangling a key from his finger.

"The Daffodil Room, second floor," he said. "It cost

me a quid. We're not to take anything. Oh, and he's expecting the constable any moment, so we had best hurry." They walked swiftly to the staircase and began climbing.

"What was her name?" she asked.

"She registered yesterday afternoon as Mrs. St. John, from London. She took the room for only the one night."

Lydia wondered if it was a coincidence, her using a variation on Sir John's name. "Did he not wonder when she didn't return to the inn last night?"

"He suspected her vocation. It is not unusual for a member of the muslin company to stay out all night."

"She would not have told him where she was going, I suppose?"

Beaumont hesitated a moment before replying, "She didn't say." Lydia looked on the verge of fainting. No need to let her know the worst.

The bedroom doors bore painted flowers to match the name of the room or suite. When they espied the daffodil, Beaumont inserted the key and they entered a spacious chamber done in daffodil yellow, with a view of the High Street through a pair of windows, one on either side of the canopied bed. The room smelled of musky perfume, powder, and stale air. A bottle of wine, half empty, and a single glass rested on the bedside table, along with a ladies' magazine. Although the bed had not been slept in, the coverlet had been pulled down and the pillows tossed aside. The room bore other traces of occupancy as well. Lydia's nostrils pinched in distaste to see such slovenly disarray.

Mrs. St. John had made a great deal of mess for someone who traveled so light. It was hard to believe that so many objects had come out of the one bandbox. The round cardboard box, covered in elegant maroon kidskin and lined in silk, had been tossed on the bed, with its lid beside it. A foam of lingerie tumbled onto the coverlet. One pink satin mule with a high heel and a puff of pink eiderdown decorating the toe was latched playfully over the rim of the bandbox. The other was on the floor halfway across the room, as if she had not just kicked it off but thrown it in a fit of temper.

On the toilet table sat an array of cosmetic bottles and boxes, along with a brush, comb, and hand mirror in chased silver. Lydia went to examine the articles, which held a strange fascination for one accustomed to seeing only a brush, comb, and talcum powder on her own and her mama's toilet tables. Face powder, rouge, perfume, nail file, manicure scissors, and assorted small articles, perhaps for arranging the coiffure, sat in a jumble on the mahogany surface. All this for one day's visit. A dusting of face powder was sprinkled over it all.

"Do you see a reticule?" Beaumont asked, lifting a drift of white, lacy peignoir and peering into the bandbox.

"No, she would have taken that with her."

"We didn't find it in the river. Perhaps whoever searched her room got it."

Lydia jerked to attention. "What do you mean, searched her room?"

"Look around you," he said, pointing at the slipper and the disarranged pillows. "Someone's been here before us. He didn't use a key. I asked the clerk if anyone had been asking for Mrs. St. John. With luck, the purse is at the bottom of the river. I'll go swimming later and dive for it." As he spoke, he continued rooting in the box. He dumped a pair of blue silk stockings onto the bed and held the box up. The silk lining had been ripped out.

Lydia just stared in silence. So Beaumont was right. The room had been searched. And she was glad, because her papa had certainly not risked exposure by coming to a public inn to meet his mistress. Someone else was involved in her murder. She suppressed the thought that it might have been an assassin hired by Sir John.

"What's the matter, Miss Trevelyn?" Beaumont asked. "You look as if you'd seen a ghost."

"Papa didn't do this," she said in a small, frightened voice.

"Good lord, I didn't think for a minute he had. Er—do you think he might have been involved with Mrs. St. John?"

"I suppose it's possible," she allowed. "He is only human after all, and being away from home so much . . ."

Beaumont just shrugged his shoulders, relieved that she had accepted the inevitable. "Where there is marriage without love, there will be love without marriage."

"But he does love us!"

"I am sure he loves you, Miss Trevelyn. You must not take this personally. Indeed, I am sure he is fond of your mama, or he would not have been at such pains to conceal from her all these years that he has a mistress. Such women are called a 'convenience' for a reason. That is all Mrs. St. John was, a convenience."

Lydia latched on to that telling "all these years." All these years her papa had been deceiving them, and Beaumont had known all about it. Very likely

22

all the gentlemen knew and were in league to hide it from the ladies. She was as close to hating her father as she had ever been to hating anyone. She felt betrayed.

"Well, she is not so convenient now, is she?" she said angrily. "We must protect Mama at all costs, Beaumont."

"I am relieved to see you acting so sensibly," he said in accents of approval. Say that for Lydia, at least she wasn't a demmed watering pot. Nor had her prudishness given her such a disgust of her father that she would go running to her mother with the tale. The news had shattered her, but she was taking it like a regular little guy.

"Of course, we are not sure Mrs. St. John was Papa's mistress," she said, darting a hopeful look at him.

"Actually, we are pretty sure," he said, wishing it were not so. "She asked for directions to Trevelyn Hall before going out yesterday afternoon. I didn't want to tell you. . . ."

He watched as her face began to crumple. Her shoulders sagged in defeat, her head drooped, and her lower lip began to tremble in a way that made Beaumont want to comfort her. He made an instinctive move toward her, but before he touched her, her head came up and he saw her face stiffen.

"Thank you for telling me, Beaumont. It is not necessary to try to protect me, you know. So, what are we to do?"

"Find out what the deuce she was doing here, and who killed her."

Her chin firmed and a martial light lit her gray eyes. "Yes, that is what I must do. Thank you for your help, Beaumont. I shall look after things from here. This is my family's problem."

His lips twitched in amusement, but his brow was furrowed. Lydia trying to straighten out this mess would be like a kitten trying to solve a problem in algebra. He was looking forward to the solving of the puzzle himself and felt no qualms whatever about his ability to do so. It would pass the time agreeably until he left for his summer house in Brighton.

"And how will you do that, Miss Trevelyn?" he asked.

"When I discover where she is from, I shall go to London and—and look into it," she said vaguely. "Speak to her friends, you know." Even as she spoke, she realized the impossibility of the thing. What excuse could she make for going to London when her father wasn't even there? How could she get away without Mama? Once there, how could she go unescorted to such places as lightskirts inhabited? She was bound in on every side by the mere fact of being a lady.

"An excellent plan," Beaumont said. "If I cannot find her reticule and her address, we shall just have to ask Sir John where she lives."

Lydia puckered her lips to say "We?" but thought again before offending Beaumont. He would be an excellent ally in her scheme. Her mama doted on him. He might even make an excuse to go to London. Some remnant of feminine guile remained with her. She smiled demurely and said, "That would be awfully kind of you, Beaumont."

Beaumont felt only an instant's gratification at her maidenly response. His chest had just begun to

24

swell when he noticed the sly smile she was trying to conceal.

"My pleasure," he said, in a voice that hinted at anything but.

Chapter Three

As the afternoon was far advanced when Lord Beaumont brought Miss Trevelyn home, the trip to London had to wait until the next morning. Anxious as Lady Trevelyn was to oblige Beaumont, she still felt constrained to utter a few objections to the scheme.

"With neither your papa nor I at the London house, my dear, who will chaperon you?" she asked her daughter.

"Why, Aunt Nessie to be sure," Lydia replied. This was Sir John's sister who kept house for him in London.

"I shall see she comes to no grief when she leaves the house, ma'am," Beaumont said with his most charming smile that invariably made the mamas wish they were twenty years younger and single.

Lady Trevelyn simpered. "Well, it is odd she would not go to London when I wanted her to and insists on going now, but that is the way with girls." She peered from her daughter to Beaumont, with curiosity gleaming from her eyes.

Lydia's blush was as good as an announcement that romance was afoot.

"Headstrong," Beaumont said, shaking his head.

26

"You know I have been wanting to attend Mr. Coleridge's lecture, Mama," the deceitful girl said.

Lady Trevelyn would have preferred a more romantic outing but poets were in vogue this season, so perhaps a lecture would not be such a dull scald as she imagined. "And Lord Beaumont has agreed to accompany you. So kind. I don't believe Sir John will object to that, when Nessie is there to see no harm comes to you. When will you be returning?"

"The day after tomorrow," Beaumont replied.

"If I stay another day, I shall write you a note, Mama," Lydia added, in case her papa's business took her a little longer.

"That might be best, dear. You will want a day to recover from the lecture." Beaumont's lips twitched at this telling speech. Lydia noticed and scowled at him. It was all right for her to find her mother a little ridiculous, but it annoyed her that someone outside the family should do so.

After he left, Lady Trevelyn had a deal more to say to her daughter, all of an admonishing nature. With all the restrictions as to propriety and remembering she was a lady, Lydia was still to let Beaumont know she was eager to become his bride.

Lydia interrupted the flow of exhortations in midstream. "It is only Beaumont, Mama, not the Prince of Wales."

"I should hope not! As if I would let you associate with that— One hears such tales of his wickedness. We shall go up and tell your papa of the visit," she said, and struggled out of her padded chair.

Lydia felt a pronounced revulsion to entering her papa's room, but she could hardly leave without seeing him, and it seemed best to do it with her mama so that she would not have to say much.

Sir John, wearing a white linen nightshirt with a ruffled neckband, was propped up in a carved bed of imperial size, curtained in red damask. The elegant chamber had been turned into an ad hoc office, with papers and documents scattered over various tables and the desk. He had a folio of government papers in front of him and a pair of spectacles perched on the end of his aquiline nose.

Lydia observed him as if he were a stranger, for so he seemed to her now. He was an elegant figure, even in his nightshirt. Age had been kind to him. The silver wings that adorned his temples lent an added air of distinction to his lean, swarthy face. As he had heard no rumor of the lightskirt's murder, it never occurred to him that there was any ulterior motive for Lydia's visit to London. He felt a match with Beaumont an excellent thing and directed a kindly smile at her as he removed his reading spectacles.

"Enjoy yourself, Lydia. I have every confidence in your good sense. I don't have to tell you not to run into trouble. Bring me my strongbox. You'll want a little pocket money."

Lydia brought the strongbox from his desk. He unlocked it and handed her a few bills of large denomination.

"Thank you, Papa," she said in a failing voice. His smile was as gentle and loving as ever and seemed genuine. How was it possible, when he had been leading a double life all this time?

Lady Trevelyn enquired dutifully how he was feeling and if there was anything the servants could do for him. He said he was feeling somewhat stouter; then the ladies rose to leave.

"Aren't you going to kiss me good night, Lydia?" he asked.

A jolt of anger smote her heart at the casual words. She had to quell the angry tirade that rose to her throat. She blew him a kiss from the door, fearing that if she touched him, she would burst into tears of frustration.

"I shan't disturb you again tonight, John," his wife said. "Good night, dear. I hope you sleep well." Lydia noticed her parents had not exchanged a kiss, nor had her papa asked his wife if she was not going to kiss him.

"Good night, dear," he replied, already putting his spectacles back on and drawing his papers forward.

After Lydia went to her room to change for dinner, it struck her as odd that her parents should say good night so early. They hadn't dined yet. It wasn't even dark out. Her mama was not going out, nor was there company coming. Did her mother know about the lightskirt? Was that why she treated her husband so coolly, hardly like a husband at all, but like a troublesome guest?

All this was so worrying that Lydia wanted to be alone to think about it. She used the excuse of packing to go up to her room immediately after dinner. It took Marie, the upstairs maid, only half an hour to pack up what was required for the short visit. When the trunk was ready, Lydia lay on her bed, looking at the window as the purple shadows of twilight dimmed to darkness. She tried to remember if she had ever seen any tokens of affection between her parents.

Her mama talked about Sir John a great deal. In theory, her life revolved around him, but when he came home from London, she just gave him a peck

29

on the cheek and asked how everything was going at Whitehall. It was Lydia herself who flew into his arms and welcomed him more warmly. She was the one who asked the more detailed questions about what he had been doing. Her mama just sat, poking her needle into whatever piece of embroidery she was working on, listening with perfect contentment. When she spoke, it was about little neighborhood doings.

When Lydia became aware that the window had turned black, she glanced at her watch and saw it was ten o'clock. She rose to go belowstairs to say good night to her mother. As she passed her father's room, she saw a stream of light coming from the partially opened door. Something in her wanted to go in and see him, but a hot, angry lump in her chest steeled her against the impulse.

"Papa is still awake, if you want to say good night to him," she mentioned to her mother when she was in the saloon.

Lady Trevelyn looked up from her embroidery and replied, "I shan't disturb him, Lydia. He will be busy with his reports."

"It wouldn't disturb him to say good night."

"Why don't you do that then, dear? I want to finish this tulip."

Lydia didn't say good night to him either. She still couldn't face him. Her sleep was troubled, but she awoke early and had been waiting half an hour before Lord Beaumont's curricle and team of matched grays drew up to the door. She had already taken leave of her mama, who usually took her breakfast in bed.

"I thought you would be taking your closed carriage," she said, surprised to see the open sporting

30

rig standing outside. She actually preferred the open carriage, but she knew her mama would dislike it. "Raffish" had been Lady Trevelyn's pronouncement when Beaumont first appeared in the dashing rig, all shining with yellow varnish and silver mountings.

Beaumont, who felt he was being chivalrous to help a damsel in distress, was miffed that her greeting should be so cool, and when he was wearing his new jacket, too. He noticed that Lydia hadn't taken any pains with her toilette. A virtual stranger to London, she dressed in the provincial fashion in a low poke bonnet with a few small flowers around the brim. Her mantle was navy worsted with some modest frogging down the front. As to dismissing his blood team with that chiding remark about the closed carriage! Dozens of ladies hinted for the privilege of sitting in his curricle.

"They are all the crack in London. Everyone drives them," he said.

"Everyone? I doubt the royal family drives such things."

"I mean everyone who is anyone," he riposted. He looked up at the blue sky, dappled with a few pearly clouds. "It's such a fine day, I thought you would enjoy the open carriage."

"You would enjoy it, you mean," she replied.

"That, too. It's a deal faster than a chaise. Sixteen miles an hour."

"It's not a race," she said. Her troubles left her short-tempered.

Beaumont was not pleased to see the small trunk the servants carried down to the carriage. "A good thing," he muttered. "What the devil are you bringing to London? We're staying only a day." He

31

helped her into the passenger's seat and took up the reins.

"I may have to stay longer. I daresay you have clothes in London. I don't. I have to bring what I may need."

He jiggled the reins, and the team set off at a lively gait, despite the trunk. With a two-hour trip to look forward to, Beaumont decided to forget the poor beginning and make some light conversation. "Why didn't you make your curtsey this past season, Lydia?" he asked.

Her first name slipped out unnoticed by either of them. Beaumont used to call her that before she let her skirts down and pinned her hair up. He had liked her better in those days. She had been just a troublesome youngster, and therefore of no romantic interest to him, but he liked her. He never imagined she would grow up into such a stiff-rumped young lady. She used to pelt through the meadows with that water spaniel trailing at her heels; she used to ride a white cob and climb trees. More than once he had had to rescue her from the old willow by the river.

"I am not on the catch for a husband," she replied.

"Isn't it about time you were? You must be—" He peered at her, trying to remember the exact difference in their ages.

"Eighteen. I wouldn't care if I were twice that. I'm not interested in marriage."

"You shouldn't let this little contretemps at home put you off," he said in an avuncular fashion that got her back up.

"Little contretemps? You call twenty years of a sham marriage a little contretemps? Twenty years of adultery? You are lenient, milord."

32

"Who says it was twenty years? The lady in the river is hardly old enough for that."

"Do you think she is his first mistress?" she asked with a sneer. "I don't. And anyway," she added, lifting her chin, "I had decided against marriage before I learned about Papa and Mrs. St. John. Why should I subject myself to a lord and master? Ladies are fools to marry, to hand their dowry over to a man, and to beg pin money from him as if they were children. Sit at home and look after the house and children—and have to bear them as well—while the man rackets around with lightskirts. Marriage is an excellent thing—for men."

Beaumont looked bored. "I've heard all this before. It is all the crack these days for ladies to claim a disinterest in marriage, but it don't stop them from leaping at the altar at the first opportunity. When it comes down to it, what is the alternative?"

"Remaining free," she said grandly.

"Remaining spinsters," he retorted. "Whatever their difficulties, married ladies have a deal more freedom than their unmarried sisters. They may go pretty well where they wish, even have affairs if that is their inclination."

"It sounds charming," she said with a withering look, "but I have no taste for lechery. I plan to do something useful with my life."

"Such as?"

"Such as finding out about this murder, to start with. Later, I shall find some worthy cause and devote myself to it."

Bored with the conversation, he said, "Did you discover anything from your papa?"

"He is not likely to say anything now, when he

33

has kept his secret from us all these years. Did you find the reticule in the river?"

"No. I dove in a dozen times and searched all along the bank as well. Perhaps the man who searched her room at the inn got it."

"I plan to search Papa's desk in London and see if I can find out about that woman—where she lives and so on. Mama and I are seldom in London, so he might have felt free to leave letters from her in his study or bedchamber."

"If you can find an address, I'll go to the house and quiz the servants. Find out who her friends were."

Lydia lifted a well-arched eyebrow and stared at him. *He* would go to her house and quiz her friends. How eager these men were to take over.

"We'll see," she said, for she didn't like to berate him when he was necessary to her trip. "I'll tell Aunt Nessie he wants me to take some papers home for him, to make an excuse to search his desk."

He lifted his eyes from the road and said playfully, "Despite your little rant, you are a complete woman, Lydia. Deceit comes naturally to you."

"You wrong women to claim deceit as a feminine vice, milord. I inherited it from my papa," she replied in a bitter voice.

"Don't be too hard on him. He spends much time alone in London."

"I doubt he spends much time alone."

"Without his wife and family, was my meaning. A man needs company."

"He has Nessie. Mama never felt the need of a boyfriend. She is away from him for weeks on end."

"By choice," he pointed out. "What is to stop her from going to London with him? Most wives do."

34

"Why should she, when he has—had that woman?"

"Which came first, the chicken or the egg?"

She tossed her curls angrily. "Naturally you would take his side."

"We men are all alike, you mean?"

"Precisely."

"I have observed your mama's experience hasn't put her off the notion of marriage. She is all in favor of your nabbing a husband. My mama tells me Lady Trevelyn was disappointed when you refused to make your debut."

"She doesn't know any better," Lydia said with a shrug of her shoulders. "It is the only life she can envisage for a lady. I have different plans."

"London is full of worthy causes. You are no longer a child. You could go to London to provide company for your papa while performing your charitable works."

"I doubt I would see much of him."

Beaumont flicked the switch over the team's head and neatly passed a donkey cart that was blocking his progress. He expected a compliment on his driving and was irritated when she said in a chiding way, "We are not going to a fire, Beaumont. For goodness' sake, drive more carefully. You'll run us into a ditch."

"Would you care to take the reins?"

He meant it as a setdown and was annoyed when she said, "I would be happy to."

"Over my dead body!"

"I happen to be an excellent fiddler! That is exactly what I mean about you—about men. They think they can do everything better," she said, and turned her head aside to examine the scenery.

"I disagree, ma'am. No one can sulk like a spoiled beauty."

Even that charge of beauty didn't interest her. Her mind was busy wondering how she could keep Beaumont from taking over the investigation when they got to London. He would try, in that odiously masculine way, to protect her. He didn't used to be so condescending when she was a child. He had treated her like an equal then. She had even got the better of him in a few contests. Skipping flat stones across the river's surface was her particular skill. Now that she was grown up, he treated her like a child.

It was not yet noon when they reached Trevelyn's house on Grosvenor Square. The house was similar to its neighbors in this gracious part of London. It was a large, three-story brick building with white pillars and an exquisitely molded door with a shining urn knocker. A lamppost crowned the stone steps leading to the door. Windows gleamed in the sunlight.

"What time will you call this afternoon?" she asked.

Beaumont blinked in surprise. He had been expecting an invitation to lunch. "What time will be convenient?" he asked.

"Give me an hour to search. I'll have to freshen up and have a bite. Come around two. If that is convenient?" she added, when she noticed his scowl.

"Your hansom cab will be here at two, milady."

"Don't be late," she said, and climbed down from her seat before he could get out to assist her. It required an unladylike leap to descend from the high perch carriage.

Beaumont was in a remarkably black humor by the time he reached his own house on Manchester Square. Rude chit. He ought to teach her a lesson.

He had a good mind not to call on her at all, except that she might find Mrs. St. John's address and go sending Bow Street off to stir up trouble or some such thing. He need not fear she would go alone in any case. Too stiff-rumped for anything so daring. The old Lydia would have done just that. And she would have invited him to join her for lunch, too. He was ravenous. At least he was rid of her for the present. He would ask some questions among his friends and see what he could discover about Sir John and his mistress.

Chapter Four

Nessie was surprised to see her niece land in unannounced and unaccompanied by either of her parents. Without knowing it, Nessie had become Lydia's model and mentor in absentia. She was a spinster who seemed perfectly happy with her lot. She had some money of her own and a busy life spent on a good cause. Her acting as Sir John's housekeeper was a favor to him. She was actually more hostess and companion for social functions than housekeeper. Her spare time and money were devoted to charitable works.

At forty-five, she had the same elegant good looks as her brother. Tall, dark-haired, with a lively, intelligent face, she wore her hair drawn high on her head in an intricate swirl. Her bronze day gown was stylish and elegant without being fussy.

"Lydia! My dear, what brings you to town? Not a toothache, I hope?"

"No indeed, Auntie," she said, and gave her aunt a hug. "I have come to hear Mr. Coleridge's lecture this evening. Beaumont brought me. He will be calling for me this afternoon—for a drive in the park."

"You should have invited him in!"

Lydia frowned. She had not thought of that. She was ready for a cup of tea herself, and no doubt Beaumont would have appreciated an ale. He had had the job of driving.

"I didn't think of it. That was remiss of me."

"No matter. Congratulations on your catch, Lydia. How did you nab him? He has been the despair of the mamas for half a dozen seasons now."

"You misunderstand the matter," Lydia said at once. She was disappointed in her aunt. She had thought her mind would be above such mundane concerns. "It is not a match. Merely Beaumont was coming to town and offered to bring me."

"And take you for a drive this afternoon and to the lecture this evening. I doubt he would do that for—say, a maiden aunt," Nessie said with a waggish smile.

"No, truly! We are just friends and neighbors. Pray do not give him the absurd notion I am throwing my bonnet at him."

"Oh indeed, no. I am not a complete flat. We must let the lad think he is doing the courting."

The ladies settled in for a little chat. As Lydia looked around the room, she was struck by how refined it was compared to her country home. Her mama favored a fussy sort of decor, with many samples of her arts of embroidery and dried flowers from a former craze. The paintings were maudlin narrative scenes, mostly of children and cats or dogs. Here all was classical elegance. The books and journals on the sofa table hinted at more intellectual pursuits than embroidery.

"What news from the Hall?" Nessie asked. "Will John be returning to London soon?"

"He says he is feeling stouter, but he is still in bed," Lydia said. As the biggest news in the parish was the death of Mrs. St. John, she decided she should mention it. She would watch for Nessie's reaction to the name.

"We have had a bit of excitement. A dead body was found in the river, just there by the bridge between the Hall and Pontneuf Chase. A Mrs. St. John."

"Oh dear," Nessie said, but she didn't say it as if she recognized the name.

"A redheaded woman. A lightskirt, they are saying. She was not a local woman. No one knows what she was doing there."

Even this did not rouse Nessie to more than casual interest. "A pity she ended up so close to your home. I daresay it has put Miriam in a pucker."

"Yes, Mama was quite upset."

They chatted for a quarter of an hour; then Lydia said, "I shall go upstairs now to freshen up. At what time is lunch?"

"What time is Beaumont coming?"

"Around two."

"Then we shall have a bite early, at one."

Lydia's trunk had been unpacked when she went to her room. The rose suite was kept for Lydia's use on those rare occasions when she visited London, usually for some formal affair such as a wedding in the family. She noticed that the servants had brought water, fresh towels, and even flowers. Nessie was such a good hostess.

Lydia didn't remain long in the room. She darted down the hall to her father's bedchamber, a smaller version of the master bedroom at home, and began rifling the desk for evidence of his liaison with

Mrs. St. John. She found nothing whatsoever. On his dresser sat a small picture in a silver frame of herself when she was ten years old. On his toilet table was an ivory miniature of her mama, looking so different from her present self. Lydia didn't remember her ever having blond curls and a dimpled smile. She was touched that her papa kept the likeness by his bed. Did he not feel like a Judas every time he looked at it?

When she heard Nessie go to her room, she ran downstairs to search the study. Its mahogany surface held only the leather-bound blotter, calendar, ink pot, and pens. On one corner of the desk sat a cardboard box. She lifted it and shook it. It was small but heavy. There was no name on it. It could hardly have anything to do with Mrs. St. John.

She began opening drawers. There, right in the little middle drawer, she found a note written on violet paper in an unformed hand. It was the same color of paper as the note Papa had pushed under the coverlet when she went into his room at home. The note was dated the day before her papa had left London. She took it up and hesitated a moment before reading it. In such dire circumstances as the present, she felt justified. She would skip over the warm bits. She read:

My Dearest John:
A wee problem has come up with Dooley. You mind I mentioned him to you. I want to get away from London for a few days. Dont worry if you come back and find me gone. You know I will never dezert you. I'll miss you. Call on me as soon as you return. Thank you for the new

bonet. Red, my favorite color! I'll wear it next
time we go out.

As ever, your Prissie.

Lydia sat a moment, simmering with fury. "My
Dearest John" was a cruel blow. The intimacy of
"your Prissie," as if she were a thing to be owned,
was even more infuriating. "You know I will never
dezert you" was the worst of all. Papa buying bonnets for that vulgar woman who could not even
spell! And who the devil was Dooley? She read it
again and again, until she had it by heart. Only
then did she realize it told her little about the hussy
except her name and her lack of education. There
was no address, not even a last name. She wondered, too, if her papa had deigned to go home only
because his mistress was leaving town.

She searched the rest of the drawers, but if
Prissie had sent more notes, her papa had not kept
them. Not here, in any case. She had hoped for an
address, that she might go there by herself and find
out about the woman. Now she would have to rely
on Beaumont. And there was really no relying on
him to tell her what he discovered.

She schooled her expression to one of polite pleasure and went to await her aunt in the saloon.
Before long, Nessie returned and they went in to
luncheon. Like the saloon, lunch was pleasingly different from the heavy, hot meals her mama favored.
A delicate consommé and an herb omelette were
more enjoyable than a chop and potatoes in the
warm weather.

"I hope you don't mind," Nessie said. "If I had
known you were coming—"

"Oh no! It's fine, Nessie. Delicious."

"The truth is, I am watching my waist. If I don't, no one else will," she said, laughing. "I'm afraid I have only fruit and cheese for dessert. I'll ask Cook to make a plum cake for dinner."

"Not on my account."

"The orange soufflé, then."

"Yes, that would be nice."

As soon as lunch was over, Nessie said, "You will want to make a fresh toilette for your outing. Even in the curricle, you can wear a more elegant bonnet in town. Beaumont will keep the pace down to a polite trot."

"I didn't bring any other bonnet," Lydia said, surprised at Nessie's concern for fashion. Yet as she considered it, Nessie had always been a stylish dresser.

"Oh dear. An out-and-outer like Beaumont won't appreciate that pokey thing you wore. Borrow one of mine, or you will look like a country mouse."

"I'm not trying to impress anyone," Lydia said.

"Then you must wear a different bonnet, or you will most unfavorably impress everyone you meet."

Lydia gave her aunt a disparaging look. "I didn't think you cared about such things, Nessie. It's so . . . feminine."

"Thank you very much, miss! You make me sound like a dowd. Everyone likes to look her best. It is not only the ladies who take care to look well. Why, the gentlemen are ten times worse. They spend hours with their tailors, discussing the cut of a lapel or sleeve. They do it to look well for us ladies. It is only fair that we return the compliment."

As Lydia didn't see how wearing a fancier bonnet would impede her search for information about Mrs.

St. John, she agreed to wear the borrowed one. When she sat in front of Nessie's mirror with a stylish concoction of feathers on her head, she was pleased with her appearance.

So was Beaumont when he called for her. "A charming chapeau, Lydia. I was afraid you planned to wear that hideous scrap of nothing you wore this morning. I would be ashamed to be seen with you," he said, smiling to show her he was joking.

She returned an icy little smile. "I had no idea you were so superficial, Beaumont."

"Clothes reflect the mind of their wearer. That is an elegant bonnet for an elegant mind. Shall we go?"

"You will join us for dinner, I hope, Beaumont?" Nessie said, pleased with the unintentional compliment to herself.

"Thank you, ma'am. I would be delighted. Eightish?"

"No, earlier!" Lydia exclaimed.

"You are not in the country now, dear," her aunt said.

"But—but the lecture begins at eight," she said.

"Oh yes, the Coleridge lecture," Nessie said. "It slipped my mind. What is the subject?"

A guilty flush started on Lydia's cheeks. She had read that Coleridge was to give a series of lectures and thought it would be interesting to attend, but as it was unlikely, she hadn't paid much attention. She cast an appealing eye on Beaumont.

"Shakespeare," he said. "Coleridge is involving himself in the controversy over whether he actually wrote his own plays. Nonsense, of course, but Coleridge likes a good argument."

44

"That should be very interesting—for blue-stockings," Nessie said with a tsk.

They made their escape soon after that little contretemps.

Lydia was disappointed to see Beaumont's crested carriage waiting at the door. No one would see her in Nessie's lovely bonnet. She immediately chided herself for this vain thought.

"Why did you change carriages?" she asked.

"You expressed disappointment that I had driven my curricle this morning. I did it to please you."

"Oh," she said, her expression making perfectly clear she was not pleased. "Thank you. That was thoughtful of you, Beaumont," she said, and climbed into the rig.

"Did you have any luck with your searching?" he asked.

"Very little, just one note, dated the day before Papa came home. Her first name is Prissie. Papa bought her a bonnet before he left. Red, like the one the lady in the river wore. She said she would be away for a few days. It is odd she didn't mention it if she was going to Kesterly."

"Perhaps she thought your papa would not like it."

"Then you think he didn't know where she was going? It is odd that he returned home himself the very next day."

"Coincidence. What else did the note say?"

"Coincidence, or did he write her and invite her?"

"I shouldn't think so," Beaumont said. "He is too sharp to foul his own nest."

"She mentioned a man named Dooley. She was having some trouble with him. She said Papa would know who she meant. Do you recognize the name?"

After a frowning pause, Beaumont said, "No, the name means nothing to me. Irish, of course."

"Oh." She sat, thinking.

"You didn't ask me what I discovered," Beaumont said, chewing back a smile of triumph.

She looked at him with interest. "Did you find out something?"

"I did. Her name was not St. John for one thing. It was Prissie Shepherd. I expect she used an alias at the inn because of its being so close to Trevelyn Hall, in case anyone who knew of her association with your papa should see her name in the register. Or perhaps she had some other reason. If she was having trouble with this Dooley fellow, she might have been trying to avoid him."

"I wonder what trouble she was in."

"Let us hope we find a clue at her apartment."

"I didn't get her address," Lydia said, and sighed.

He gave her a triumphant little smile. "I did."

"Where? How?"

"From a friend."

Her eagerness faded to chagrin. "Then everyone knows about her and Papa?"

"There are few secrets in London, but the friend I got it from is not one of the everyones you are concerned about. It wasn't Prinny. It was a lightskirt."

She pokered up. "I see. How—convenient that you know women like that."

"Yes, wasn't it?" he replied, refusing to take offense. Lydia Trevelyn had become a demmed prude, and it was time someone opened up her eyes. "They make a pleasant change from prudes and bores," he said.

"Are you saying Mama is a prude and a bore?"

He directed a pointed look at her. "No, not your mama," he said.

It was Lydia's turn not to take offense—or to pretend not to. "What is the address?" she asked.

"Maddox Street, just off New Bond."

"That must cost Papa a good deal."

"It's hardly a lavish address. Is it the money he spends on her you resent?"

"He was very happy when I didn't want to come to make my debut in April. He said he was a little short. No wonder!"

"A mistress is cheaper than gambling. A man must have some relaxation."

"Does it have to be a degrading relaxation? Did they never hear of books?" she said angrily.

"Books are a fine adjunct to living. They are hardly a replacement for it, even at Sir John's age. For youngsters," he added with a meaningful look, "they are either a waste of time if one reads trashy novels—"

"I do not read trashy novels!"

"You didn't allow me to finish. There is a time for things. The time to read good literature or philosophy is after one has lived a little. Otherwise, such heavy stuff is pretty well meaningless. One has no frame of reference to understand them."

Lydia sat digesting this while they drove to Maddox Street. It was true she could not make heads or tails of half the stuff she read. It occurred to her that she spent an inordinate amount of time with her nose in a book or journal, not living but reading about life. If she had been more in the world, she would know about such things as mistresses and gambling. She would have realized the

47

temptation her papa faced, and urged her mama to go to London and keep an eye on him.

"I believe you're right, Beaumont," she said with a glint he could not quite trust in her eyes. "It is time I started living."

Chapter Five

The brown brick house on Maddox Street was not grand enough to infuriate Lydia, but it was by no means derelict, and it was enormous. "Look at the size of it!" she cried. "It must require dozens of servants."

"Many of these houses have been divided into flats," Beaumont explained.

They left the carriage and went to the front door, where a discreet sign indicated there were four households within, two downstairs and two above. Miss Shepherd occupied flat 2A downstairs. Beaumont tried the front door and they entered a small, tiled foyer with a staircase leading to the next story and doors on either end. The door on the right said 2A. A tap of the acorn knocker brought no servant to admit them. When they tried the door, it was locked.

As there was no one about, Beaumont drew out a clasp knife and began to work on the lock. When the blade didn't work, he tried the corkscrew. After five minutes, he said, "I'll go around to the back and see if I can force a window open."

Lydia removed a nail file from her reticule and took a turn at the lock. Beaumont watched her work for a moment, then went out the front door, assured that she would not succeed where he had failed. When he reached the back window, Lydia was there, waiting for him. She unlocked the window and leaned out.

"Do you want to go around to the door, or come in this way?" she enquired with a triumphant smile that annoyed him to no small degree.

He clambered into a spotless kitchen without acknowledging verbally that she had outdone him.

"We'll have to move quickly," he said. "The servants may return at any moment."

"There is no one staying here."

"My dear girl, an empty flat does not mean—"

"No, but an empty larder does. There is no milk, no butter, no eggs. The stove is cold, and in fact, there is a film of dust on the kettle. I believe Prissie gave her servant a holiday before she left."

"I see. Then it seems you're right," he said grudgingly.

She went to the window behind him and closed it.

"Leave it open a crack in case—"

She gave him an impatient look. Glancing at the window, he saw she had left it open an inch at the bottom to facilitate entrance in case they should want to return.

"You must not assume, just because I am a female, that I am an idiot, Beaumont," she said, and strode out of the kitchen with her head high and her back as stiff as a board. She continued along a corridor to the parlor, which was not large or grand enough to be called a saloon.

In style, the decor was closer to Trevelyn Hall than the house on Grosvenor Square. Lydia thought her papa must have felt quite at home here, with all those dried flowers and the surfeit of ornaments on the wall. Though not even her mama would have permitted that garish red-and-blue-patterned carpet with a green-and-yellow-striped sofa. One wall held watercolors, mostly of smiling young women. The opposite wall was hung with decorative plates from various resorts. Tunbridge Wells, Brighton, Weymouth. The sort of thing tourists bought because they were there, and had the sense to consign to a cupboard or put a potted plant on when they got home.

Half a dozen fashion magazines were fanned out on the sofa table beside an empty wine decanter and a crystal bonbon dish with a domed lid. There was nothing to indicate a more serious turn of mind. No books, no journals. What on earth had attracted her papa to such a woman? He was intelligent, worldly, worked with the most important gentlemen in England—and came to this tawdry place for his amusement.

She just shook her head and continued her exploration. One door led her to a spartan chamber that was obviously a maid's room. Across the hall she saw Beaumont standing at a clothespress, examining the gowns. She went to the bedroom and stood, gazing around. It was done in white and pink and reminded her of a birthday present. A large bed occupied one corner. Flounces of white lace formed the canopy and seemed to drape the entire bed. A tumble of small pink satin cushions were at the head of the bed. As Lydia walked toward it, she noticed a strong scent of that same musky perfume she had smelled in Prissie's room at the inn.

A mental picture of her father and Prissie on that bed caused her to wince and turn quickly away. On the other side of the chamber, a pink damask chaise longue sat by the grate with a white-and-gold table in the French style beside it. The dresser and desk matched the table. A telltale shaving set and a gentleman's brushes rested beside the feminine cosmetics and brushes on the toilet table. At the clothespress, Beaumont continued rooting through the gowns. Lydia went up behind him, looking for jackets. She didn't see any. He took out some black, filmy thing and held up the skirt.

"What on earth is that?" she asked.

"It is a black lace peignoir. Rather dashing."

"I didn't realize there was such a thing as a mourning peignoir."

"It is an evening peignoir, I should think."

"I meant mourning, with a *u*, as in bereavement."

"Black has more interesting associations as well."

She lifted an eyebrow in derision. "I was joking, actually."

"Ah, that is a change. You don't usually show much sense of humor."

She glared and said in a tight voice, "Unlike you, I fail to see the humor in this appalling situation."

"Point taken," he said at once, mentally berating himself for insensitivity. All this was a rude awakening for Lydia. She had always adored her papa.

He moved to the dresser and began flipping through the silken dainties there: satin nightgowns, embroidered lingerie, silk stockings in various shades.

"Such extravagance!" Lydia complained.

Her harping on the money Sir John spent on his woman annoyed him. The Trevelyns were far from poor. Lydia lacked for nothing. He looked over his shoulder with a quizzing smile. "Am I to assume Miss Trevelyn does not wear such alluring under-pinnings?" His eyes traveled in a leisurely manner from her bonnet to her toes.

"This is hardly fit conversation for mixed company. I doubt anyone but a lightskirt would wear such things. And please do not look at me like that, as if you were imagining—all sorts of things."

"Even the imagination fails at what you are suggesting." She tossed her head. "You must admit, though, Miss Shepherd has good taste."

"Good taste! She has squandered a good deal of Papa's money to very poor effect. The parlor looks as if it were put together by a color-blind twelve-year-old. As to that black peignoir!"

Beaumont refused to admit he found the flat in poor taste. "A certain country charm," he said. "The engravings are good." He waved his hand toward a folder that rested on the desk in the corner.

Lydia went to it and began to examine the folder's contents. They were at startling variance with the rest of the flat. She stared at three austere sketches, exquisitely executed on old, yellowed parchment. One was of an old man with a beard, one of an owl, and one of a crouching rabbit.

"Albrecht Dürer," Beaumont said, with a question in his voice. "A sixteenth-century artist."

"Yes, German, I believe," she added, to let him know she also recognized the pieces. "These must be Papa's. I wager he gave them to her. She wouldn't appreciate them. You notice she didn't hang them up."

"They wouldn't really suit this bower of bliss," he said, waving his hand around the ultra-feminine room.

"No, they wouldn't. They are too refined. I have a good mind to take them with me."

Beaumont went to her side and began examining the pieces more closely. He held one up to the window and frowned. "And how would you explain to your father that you have them in your possession?" he asked, replacing the sketch.

She scowled and put them back in the folder. She drew open the desk drawer and saw art paper. The other drawers held boxes of pens and nibs, charcoal, India ink, and paints.

"I believe Prissie is an artist!" she exclaimed. "I wager she painted those horrid things in the parlor herself."

She darted back into the parlor and examined the pictures hanging on the wall. They were watercolors of women and one of a young boy, all well done as to craftsmanship. They obviously depicted real, recognizable people, but they were only illustrations. They lacked that special something, that depth and integrity that would make them art. In the corner of each picture she had signed "P. Shepherd."

The discovery that Prissie was an artist was oddly disconcerting. It no longer seemed possible to consider her as just a lightskirt. She was taking on a definite personality. The white-and-pink bedroom and the expensive lingerie revealed a sensual side to her nature, but this saloon was completely different. It was the work of a homebody.

Lydia pictured her sitting in this cozy little parlor—it was cozy, if not elegant—with one of those smiling ladies in the frames, chatting as she made her sketch. What would they talk about? Their patrons? Their new gowns, their black lace peignoirs? Would they, like her mama and Lady Beaumont, gossip about their friends and servants? Who had been jilted, who had contracted a good match, and what Cook was making for dinner tonight? Were all women sisters under the skin? Even Nessie, her model, had spoken only of matches and food and fashion that morning.

She looked up when Beaumont entered the room. "Prissie painted all these," she said, indicating the watercolors.

He went forward and examined them. "I recognize this one!" he said, pointing at a sketch of a blonde with green eyes.

"Maybe we could talk to her."

"She's no longer in town. I met—saw her a few years ago. She married a fellow and moved to Ireland."

"Oh, too bad. Did you find anything else in the desk?" she asked. "I am thinking of this Dooley that Prissie was worried about."

"I found this," he said, holding out a little appointment book bound in red Morocco leather. "Dooley's name occurs frequently, but with no address. Perhaps he met her here."

"A lover, you mean?"

"Possibly your papa's predecessor—and unhappy with being jilted. That seems unlikely, though. She had been under Sir John's protection for the better part of a decade."

"How do you know that?" she asked at once.

Beaumont regretted that he had let that slip out. "It is what I heard from friends."

"Ever since I was eight years old," Lydia said in a sad, faraway voice. She was thinking of her sixteenth birthday, when he had promised to be home

55

for her party and hadn't come. He had sent her a string of pearls and a note of apology, claiming urgent business at the House. She had felt sorry for him, working so hard. He hadn't been home for any of her birthdays since then or Mama's either. "Too busy in the House" was always his excuse, but he wasn't too busy to visit Prissie Shepherd. This house on Maddox Street was "the House" that kept him occupied.

"There's no more to discover here," Beaumont said. "Let us have that drive in the park. It will cheer you up."

She gave him a questioning look. "If you think you are going to palm me off with a drive in the park, Beau, you have another think coming. I have already told Nessie we are going out this evening."

"That was not why I said it! Why are you so suspicious? I just wanted to cheer you up, you look so . . . morbid. I have nothing better to do this evening, with the Season over."

"I suppose you know a few women you would be happy to visit."

That disparaging "women" told him what sort of women she meant. If she had meant ladies, she would have said so. In other words, she was charging him with having a lightskirt. He didn't, at the moment, but he would certainly have to meet Prissie's friends if he hoped to discover who this Dooley person was.

"I am a bachelor, you know," he reminded her. "The muslin company's doors are open till dawn, which is why they're called ladies of the night. I shall do the pretty with Nessie and you first. Do you want to attend that lecture?"

"Let us try to think of something more useful we could do. Since Dooley or someone searched her room at the inn in Kesterly, he might search her room here in London as well. If we watch, we might catch him in the act."

"Unless he got what he was after at the inn," he said.

"Yes, that's possible. What could it be? Money?"

"Incriminating letters, perhaps. Love letters, I mean. I may be wronging Prissie. I don't know that she is the kind who would hold a gent to ransom over his indiscretions, but it must be something of that sort." He looked again at the sketches on the wall.

"Do you think you have met—er, seen that one as well?" she asked as his gaze settled on a redhead.

"No, I wouldn't forget a redhead with brown eyes. I was thinking of something else. Those Dürer sketches . . . The parchment didn't seem quite right. Do you think it's possible Prissie did them?"

"Forgeries, you mean? I doubt she could do such a good job."

"It might explain what Dooley was after."

"No, they wouldn't fit in her bandbox, and he—or someone—had torn the lining out of it. It's something else. I vote for billets-doux."

"You're probably right."

They took a last look around the parlor and went back out to the carriage for a drive through Hyde Park. The fair weather continued. Sunlight shone from the blue sky; greenery stretched all around them. The crush of the formal Season was over but there were still several handsome carriages at the barrier for the ritual meeting of the ton at four o'clock. Many of the occupants greeted Beaumont and looked with interest at Miss Trevelyn. One of the gentlemen dismounted from his curricle and came to their carriage. He was a tall fellow with blond curls and blue eyes. Beaumont introduced him as Lord Farnworth.

"My sister is having a little party tonight, Beau," he said. "Be very pleased if you and Miss Trevelyn would join us. Nothing formal. Just a few friends, a bit of dancing. Didn't know you was in town or I would have called sooner."

"I am just here for a few days on business," Beaumont said. He noticed Lydia looked interested, however, and asked her opinion.

She was not so keen a follower of Mary Wollstonecraft that she had not occasionally regretted missing her Season. And since Beaumont had made that remark about books being only an adjunct to life, she had begun to think she would make her curtsey next Season.

"We were going to attend Mr. Coleridge's lecture," she said, but she said it with very little enthusiasm.

"Dash it, you can hear that prosey old bore anytime. He is never so happy as when he has a captive audience," Farnsworth said.

"That is true. Very well, I should like to go, Lord Farnsworth. Thank you," she said, with a more flirtatious smile than Beaumont had won, with all his efforts on her behalf.

"See you around nine, then. Delighted to have made your acquaintance, ma'am. Beau knows where we live."

After he had left, she said to Beaumont, "I daresay you would prefer the party to a dull lecture."

"To a *dull* lecture, yes. Whether Coleridge is dull, however, is a matter of opinion. And in any case, I thought we were going to watch Prissie's flat."

"It is not too late to change our minds about the party," she said at once. "A note to Miss Farnsworth . . ."

"Cut line, Lydia. You are dying to go to that party. Why should your papa have all the fun? We can watch the flat later. I doubt Dooley would search it early in the evening. If either of us is struck by an idea as to how else we can find him, we can leave early."

"Very true, though I haven't a stitch to wear."

This feminine comment brought a twinkle to his eyes. "In that case, your success is guaranteed. You will certainly be the belle of the ball."

"Lecher!" she charged, but she could not quite hold her lips steady. It was too ludicrous to think of barging into a polite party in her birthday suit.

"You're the one who's planning to attend the party naked. Personally, I think you should wear a fig leaf." Then he paused and let his eyes drift over her body. "Or two—no, make that three," he said.

"Really, Beaumont!" she felt obliged to object. Her cheeks were flushed with embarrassment, but she was no longer wearing that prim, prudish expression.

"Yes, really," he said, pretending to misunderstand her tone. "Fig leaves are worn in all the better pictures of Adam and Eve."

She got her emotions under control and gave him a cool glance. "Shall we go now?"

"Shall I bring the leaves this evening, or will you—"

"We have worn this poor joke into the ground,"

she said stiffly, then spoiled her prudish pose by adding, "I really *don't* have anything decent to wear."

Chapter Six

Nessie was delighted to hear a party had been substituted for the Coleridge lecture. Much as she liked Lydia, she could not imagine the dashing Beaumont offering for a bluestocking, and Lydia's conversation was taking on a noticeable tinge of blue. Nessie blamed it on that book she had given Lydia last Christmas. Pity it hadn't been a subscription to *La Belle Assemblée*. Her toilette had fallen into a dangerously unfashionable state.

"Mary Wollstonecraft's book opened up my eyes, I can tell you," Lydia said, when Nessie came to her room for a chat before dinner. "I want nothing to do with gentlemen. They only want to keep our minds fettered. You chose wisely. I shall be an independent spinster like you, Nessie."

"I did not choose spinsterhood, goose," Nessie said, horrified. "The gentleman I loved did not care for me, and I could not care for the few gents who proposed to me. I would have married in the twinkling of a bedpost if the right man had asked, and been better off, too. I regret every day of my life that I did not marry and have children. What else is a woman put on earth for, but to have a family?"

"There are plenty of other things a lady can do—

61

good, useful things. Helping the poor, expanding her mind."

"Does marriage prevent her from doing that as well? Marriage doesn't mean one has to store her brain away in cotton wool and let her husband think for her. That was not Mary Wollstonecraft's meaning. You may be sure she married—and not wisely either. The trick is to marry the right sort of gentleman."

Lydia considered this and asked, "What sort do you mean?"

"The sensible sort who does not treat you like a child. Now, enough of that for the present. What will you wear to the party?"

Lydia held up a blue taffeta gown that was poorly cut and badly trimmed. "I brought this evening frock with me."

Nessie looked at it and said, "Oh yes, that would be fine for a lecture. Pity you hadn't realized there was to be a party, or you would have brought a fancier gown."

When she stood in front of the mirror, Lydia had a sinking sensation the blue gown would look dowdy beside the gowns of the other ladies at the party. Even at home it had caused very little stir. She assured herself it didn't matter in the least. It was superficial to worry about such things, but still the frock looked dowdy. She could see it in Nessie's eyes, and she saw it again in Beaumont's when he arrived for dinner.

To add to her chagrin, Nessie's gown was extremely stylish. With her black hair in a chignon and pearls at her throat, she looked sophisticated and nearly beautiful, and made Lydia feel lumpish. She noticed Beaumont gazing in admiration at

Nessie over dinner. The two of them kept up a bantering conversation, half of which flew over Lydia's head.

Of course, Beaumont was too polite to say anything about her own toilette, but as soon as dinner was over and they left for the party, she said in an aggrieved voice, "You need not look at me like that. I didn't know we would be attending a party or I would have brought a different gown."

"I see nothing amiss with the gown," he said politely. "If I betrayed any dissatisfaction, it is that scowl you wore that caused it."

"It is the gown that caused the scowl, so it amounts to the same thing."

"Try to talk sense to a woman! There is as fine a piece of sophistry as I have heard this age. It might ease your mind to learn men don't give a brass farthing about a lady's gown, Lydia. I couldn't tell you a single outfit Miss Lawrence wore last Season, but I could describe her sooty eyelashes and her pearly white teeth and her dimples to a nicety. Lovely eyes she had. Blue, but with little flecks of silvery gray in them. I never saw such eyes."

This detailed praise of Miss Lawrence did not improve Lydia's temper one whit. "Is Miss Lawrence a lightskirt?" she enquired demurely. "All those dimples and sooty eyelashes sound quite like one of Prissie's sketches."

"I hardly think the Duke of Arnprior would marry a lightskirt. Miss Lawrence nabbed him, and she had only ten thousand dowry. That usually buys no more than a baronet. Of course, Miss Lawrence's beauty is priceless."

"What does a duke usually cost?"

"Twenty-five thousand is the customary sum."

"Then Miss Lawrence's beauty is not priceless. It is worth fifteen thousand pounds."

Beaumont gave a reluctant chuckle. "You have a good head for ciphering, Lydia. I think you would have hammered out a good bargain at the Marriage Mart."

"No doubt, but I chose not to auction myself off to the highest bidder."

To tease her, he said, "Pity," and shook his head, as if he were personally disappointed to hear it.

From the corner of his eye, he noticed her head flew around to look at him. He expected some argumentative response, but she just sat, thinking. Nessie regretted not having married. What if she came to regret it, too, when it was too late? Marriage to the right gentleman did not preclude living that full mental life she aspired to.

At the party, Lord Farnsworth seemed to like Lydia despite her blue gown. When she smiled and fluttered her eyelashes at him to test Beaumont's theory, he looked quite besotted and asked her if he might call the next afternoon. Due to the exigencies of her mission, she had to decline. Sir James Harcourt also expressed an interest in calling. All the attention left her in a strangely euphoric mood, and reinforced that Beaumont knew something of the world. She told herself none of this masculine attention meant a thing. She might remain single, but still it was comforting to know that gentlemen found her attractive, that she could marry if she wished. But it was disconcerting to learn that men, who ruled the world, were such fools as to be blinded by an insincere smile and a pair of fluttering eyelashes.

The party was so enjoyable that when Beaumont

joined her at eleven-thirty and suggested rather brusquely that they should leave if she could tear herself away from Farnsworth, she was not at all eager to go.

"They will be serving supper in half an hour," she said.

"And we shall be enjoying lobster patties and champagne while Dooley walks off with the Dürer forgeries. I wager that is what he was looking for at the inn."

"They wouldn't fit in the bandbox."

He assumed an air of indifference and said, "You stay here, if you like, and enjoy the party. I'll run along to Maddox Street and come back for you later."

"No! No, he is my papa. I'll go with you, but I don't see what difference half an hour makes." She pouted and added, "I am just in the mood for champagne."

"Then stay," he said grimly.

They left at once.

"It was a lovely party," she said, as they drove at a smart clip toward Maddox Street. "Lord Farnsworth is very charming, is he not?"

"Yes, charming," he said stiffly. "And well to grass, too. Not that his fortune would be of any interest to a determined spinster."

"Oh, of course not. I was merely discussing his personality. Spinsters have friends, you know. I don't plan to retire to a convent after all."

"I should hope not! A flirting nun would be scandalous."

"I was not flirting!"

"You behaved little better than a coquette."

"I had to do something to distract attention from this horrid gown."

"Rationalizer!"

As she was not sure what the word meant, she just tossed her head and looked out the window. They could see as they drove toward Prissie's house that no lights burned in her flat. Beaumont told his coachman to drive around the block and return in a quarter of an hour. They went together down the cobbled path to the back of the house. It was dark and frightening at night. Lydia peered into the shadows, expecting someone to jump out and strike her at any moment. When a swaying branch caused a shadow to loom, she moved closer to Beaumont and held on to his arm.

"Afraid?" he asked, grinning.

"Certainly not! The cobblestones are rough. If you were a proper gentleman you would have offered me your arm."

"If I weren't afraid of getting my head bitten off, I would have done it. I thought you liked to take care of yourself."

"I do take care of myself! That doesn't mean one must ignore the social conventions."

"Only when it suits you," he replied.

At the kitchen window, they stopped and exchanged a look. The window was wide open.

"Someone's been here!" Lydia whispered.

"I'll go in and have a look."

She caught at his sleeve. "No, he might still be in there. I'll go around and tap at the front door. I'll rattle my nail file in the lock to make him think I'm coming in. He'll leave by this window, and you can catch him on the way out."

Beaumont said, "A good plan," in a brusque way, as if he disliked to admit it.

"I told you I'm not an idiot," she said, and hurried back along the dark passage, around to the front door. She did as she had said, but no one scampered out the back window.

When she rejoined Beaumont, he said, "It's safe. No one's in there—I hope."

As Lydia was shorter than he, he had to boost her up to the window; then he scrambled in behind her.

"Should we light a lamp?" she whispered.

"Let us tiptoe about a little first. See if you can find a poker. I'll take this stick of wood." He helped himself to a small log from the basket of wood by the stove, Lydia found the poker, and together they walked along the corridor, stopping often to listen for sounds from beyond.

By the time they reached the parlor, they were convinced there was no one in the flat and lit a lamp. First they looked all around the room. As at the inn, the place had been searched. The sofa was pushed aside, the pictures askew.

"The Dürer sketches!" Beaumont cried, and ran toward the bedroom.

The search here had been more detailed. The bedcoverings had been ripped off, drawers hung open with clothing tumbled to the floor, but the Dürer sketches were still in the folder.

"That's odd!" he said. "I was sure this was what he was after."

"I told you—"

"I know. They wouldn't fit in the damned box."

"You mean bandbox."

"Damned bandbox is what I mean."

"There is no need to fly into a pelter, Beaumont. I begin to think we must take the bull by the horns."

"Unfortunately, the bull has fled, taking his horns with him."

"Talk to Papa, I mean. Prissie told him about Dooley. He must know what this is all about."

"I'll take you home tomorrow, then."

"No, no. We cannot both leave. You go home and talk to Papa and let me know what he says. I shall stay here and see what I can discover on my own."

"What can you possibly do here?"

"Keep an eye on things," she said vaguely.

Beaumont looked at her askance. He didn't trust that scheming light in her eye. "I can hardly ask Sir John the necessary questions. He'll know I've been prying into his private life, reading his billets-doux. It is none of my concern, and so he would tell me in short order."

"I certainly cannot ask my own papa about his mistress! He'd box my ears and send me to my room."

"Then we have reached an impasse."

Lydia stood a minute, deep in concentration. "You mentioned Dooley's name in Prissie's address book. Were there any other names that looked promising?"

"Promising?" he asked. "There was no entry that said 'dangerous man,' or 'murderer.'"

"There is no need to snap my head off. Did any name occur frequently? We might be able to trace them and—and learn something," she said.

"She used only first names for the most part. There were no addresses, just names."

"Hmmm. You said Dooley probably met her here.

68

If that is so, then the neighbors might know something about him."

"Yes, that's true. I'll drop by tomorrow and see if I can strike up an acquaintance with one of the other lightskirts."

"Drop by where?"

"Here. These flats are very likely all filled by the muslin company. When they move in, the other occupants have a way of moving out."

"We shall come back tomorrow morning, then."

"We?" he asked, and laughed. "If you think I plan to introduce you to a parcel of lightskirts, you are very much mistaken, Lydia. I shall come alone, and let you know what I discover."

Her heart pumped faster at this overbearing speech. "What time will you call? On me, I mean?" she asked coolly.

"Five-ish. The girls tend to sleep till noon or later. Give me a couple of hours to gain their confidence. I should have something by five."

Lydia opened her lips to object, then closed them again. It was clear Beaumont planned to take over, leaving her out of all the excitement. Furthermore, if he discovered anything truly scandalous, he would keep it from her. It was kind of him to have brought her to London, but now that she was here, she would do a little work on her own.

"Very well. Thank you, Beaumont," she said, and they left, again by the kitchen window.

Beaumont climbed out first to help Lydia out, and catch her when she landed. He hoped for a little flirtation when he held her in his arms. She seemed in a mood for it tonight, to judge by her behavior at the party. She was not in the mood for flirting with Beaumont, however. He twirled her around in the air when he caught her. "You're light as a feather," he said, to make her aware of his strength.

"Put me down!" she said angrily. "You nearly bumped my head on that tree."

As the tree was some five yards away, he said, "What a big head you have!" and put her down with a thump.

When he delivered her to her front door, he said, "You might want to write your mama a note explaining that you will be staying another day. If I get a line on Dooley, as I hope, you will want to be here. I'll discuss with you what is best to be done."

"Yes, do keep me informed, Beaumont."

"What will you do during the day?" he asked.

"A pity I refused to let Farnsworth call."

"You could drop his sister Maggie a note. You ladies enjoy visiting the shops."

She, being a mere lady, was to idle away her time shopping at Vanity Fair while he, the gentleman, attended to the more important matter.

"Perhaps Nessie would like to go," she said, in a very civil voice. She thanked him again and went into the house.

Beaumont stood a moment on the curb, frowning. Lydia was proving a more complicated lady than he remembered. She claimed no interest in marriage and flirted her head off with Farnsworth. She cut up stiff when he tried to flirt with her, and had been suspiciously acquiescent to his continuing the investigation alone on the morrow. He had expected an argument about his going alone to Maddox Street. Apparently she realized it was totally ineligible for a young lady to visit lightskirts. Or perhaps that prudish side of her disliked the notion. In any case, he told himself, he was glad she would not be there to hamper his activities—though actually she had helped once or twice with the details.

Nessie was playing cards with a group of friends when Lydia went inside. She introduced Lydia, who went up to her room very soon afterward. There she paced to and fro, planning how to discover who Dooley was and what business he had with Prissie. She felt the other girls on Maddox Street must be Prissie's friends. If no one else except their patrons visited them, then obviously the girls would have formed a close group. Those sketches in Prissie's parlor suggested it. She must talk to those girls. They would not all sleep until noon. She would go earlier, about ten, and see if she could find one of them awake. And when Beaumont came to tell her what he had discovered, she would show him who was the better worker.

Going to Maddox Street required an excuse to Nessie, who would certainly insist on accompanying her if she claimed she was going shopping. After a few moments' pacing, she remembered a friend, Irene Coltrane, who had come to make her bows. She would say she was calling on Irene.

When all this was settled in her mind, she went to her papa's bedchamber and looked again at those pictures. She was glad he didn't have one of Prissie. At least the woman had not invaded the sanctity of his home, even in effigy. She lay awake a long time, wondering how her papa had met the woman, and what wiles Prissie had used to attach him. Was it simply a matter of batting her eyelashes and letting him think he was marvelous? Could men possibly be that gullible? She didn't think Beaumont would be, but with a memory of Farnsworth and Sir James, she concluded that many men were. It might prove a useful piece of information. At length, she slept.

Chapter Seven

Luck was with Lydia. The next morning, Nessie told her she had to visit Lady Melbourne regarding an orphans' charity in which she was involved, but she would be home for luncheon.

"I shall tell Lady Melbourne I cannot stay."

"Oh no, Nessie. Do stay. Beau will be calling for me in the afternoon."

"Indeed! I am delighted to hear it. But what will you do in the morning?"

"I had arranged to visit an old friend, Irene Coltrane."

"I'll send the carriage back for you, then."

"Miss Coltrane will send her carriage for me," Lydia lied. She preferred to arrive at Maddox Street in a hired cab, in case the coachman should report back to her chaperon.

As soon as Nessie left, Lydia dispatched a note home telling her mama she would be remaining for a day or two. She admitted to missing the Coleridge lecture, knowing her mama would be delighted that she had attended a party with Beaumont instead.

It was nearly eleven o'clock by the time she got out of the house and hailed a hansom to take her to Maddox Street. She went to the front door, knocked, and when there was no reply, admitted herself with her nail file. She took a quick look around to make sure the flat was unoccupied before setting to work. The disheveled apartment was just as it had been the night before, which suggested that whoever had searched it had not returned. She picked up the pillows and straightened the pictures.

Even Kesterly had its lightskirts, and Lydia knew they would not be forthcoming to a lady. It was therefore necessary that she become a temporary member of the muslin company. To this end, she went to Prissie's bedchamber and sorted through her gowns until she found a blue-sprigged muslin that nearly fit her. It was at the back of the clothespress, somewhat wrinkled and a size smaller than the newer gowns, which suggested it was from a former season.

She put the sprigged muslin on, hung her own clothes at the back of the clothespress, and went to the toilet table. Prissie had taken her cosmetics with her, but there were still some odds and ends to work with. She carefully applied a little rouge to her cheeks. Her coiffure proved more difficult to handle. Her hair was fine and silky and impossible to turn into a lightskirt's coiffure on short notice. She selected a brilliant red ribbon, tied it around her head, and made a bow at the front.

When she looked sufficiently tawdry, she went into the parlor, planning to call on her nearest neighbor. Before she opened the door, there was a tap at it. Lydia flew into a panic. What if it was Dooley or some other man with evil intent? She was about to run for the kitchen window when a woman's voice called.

"Is that you, Prissie? It's me, Sally."

Lydia stood a moment, calming herself, then went

to the door. A pretty girl not much older than herself stood there, peering in with the greatest curiosity. Sally looked like a farm girl, with glossy chestnut curls, red apple cheeks, and friendly brown eyes. It was hard to credit she was a lightskirt, but the cut of her gown and the surfeit of baubles on her wrists and fingers did not speak of the country.

"Is Prissie back yet?" she asked.

"No, she's not, but do come in. I'm happy to meet you, Sally. Prissie has told me about you."

"You'd be Nancy, then?"

"Yes," she said, smiling and ushering Sally in, and wondering who Nancy was.

"I heard you moving about in here and thought you was Prissie come back. Have you seen your sister lately?"

Sister! So that is who Nancy was. "No, but she didn't know just when I was coming, so I let myself in," she said vaguely. Sally didn't think to enquire how she had done this.

"I hope nothing's happened to her," Sally said, staring in consternation.

"I hope not indeed. When do you think she'll be back?"

They sat down on the sofa. "She was going to visit her son for his birthday, but she did say she might stay a few days if he was feeling poorly. That cough of his hangs on so."

This casual mention of a son sent Lydia's mind reeling. Was this son her half brother? She wanted to ask a hundred questions, but first she had to learn how much Nancy might be expected to know. If she lived in London, too, then she would know all Prissie's doings.

"Poor fellow," Lydia said. "I hope it's not serious."

"Just a cold, I wager, but you know Prissie. She thinks the sun rises and sets on her boy. Sir John, Richie, and her art, that's the sum and total of Prissie's life. I hope the lad ain't really sick. It looks bad, don't it, her staying away so long?"

"Indeed it does. I wonder if I should go to her." She hoped this might call forth the destination, as indeed it did.

"It wouldn't take long. St. John's Wood is only a few miles away. Prissie goes every Sunday. Mind you, it'd cost, taking a hansom."

St. John's Wood. Lydia stored up the fact, and as she did so, it occurred to her that a little orphan boy would be waiting to see his mother, who would not be coming back. She pinched her lips to steady them.

Sally gave her a comforting pat on the shoulder. "Never you mind, now, Nancy. Prissie often stays a day or two with the Nevils, just to be with her boy. With his birthday this week and Sir John away, she's likely decided to stay. That's what it is, count on it."

"I daresay," Lydia said, blinking back a tear. "How old will Richie be on his birthday? I've lost track." She did not lose track of the name Nevil, but put it away for future use.

"He must be nine or ten by now, eh? She bought him that sailor suit he liked so much the year I moved here. Lord, how time flies."

Lydia wondered if her father was also the boy's father. Prissie had been under his protection for approximately a decade, so it seemed likely. He would have to take charge of the boy if that were the case. What would he do with him? Would he claim him to be some relative's orphan and bring him to Trevelyn Hall? Meanwhile, she wanted to discover something about Dooley. As it was possible that Prissie's sister knew about him, however, she had to tread carefully.

"How's your ma?" Sally asked, looking around the room at the pictures. One of them was of herself, posing with her finger coyly holding up her chin.

"Fine."

"Did she like the muslin Prissie sent?"

"Yes, very much." Lydia took note that Prissie was a dutiful daughter, sending her mama presents.

"That's not a piece of it you're wearing, is it?"

"No, this isn't it."

"I thought she said pink."

"This is an old gown of Prissie's. She gave it to me."

"You won't be wearing hand-me-downs for long, Nance. We'll find a fellow for you, if that's why you came," she said, looking for an answer. Lydia nodded, aware that her cheeks were warm with shame. "What sort do you like?"

"Rich," Lydia said, and gave a nervous laugh. Surely the lightskirts were only interested in money.

"And handsome as well, I suppose!" Sally said jeeringly. "Lord, you'll be lucky if you get one that don't beat you. The young bucks are just after one thing, and as soon as they see a girl they like better, they run off and leave you high and dry. When all's said and done, you're better off with an older gent. Take Sir John, now." Lydia came to sharp attention. "He treats your sister like a princess, Nancy. He's that fond of her. Well, it stands to reason, with a wife like he's got, that leaves him alone all year, he's happy to have someone pay a little attention to him."

77

"Does he tell Prissie about his wife?" Lydia asked, but almost hoped the answer was negative.

"Only that he'd never leave her, nor do nothing to hurt her or his two kids. He has two kids, a son and a daughter. Not that Prissie ever expects him to marry her. Still, after all this time, it's practically a marriage, innit?"

"It sounds like it." Someone to pay a little attention to him. How sad, that her papa had to pay for a little attention.

"I say, Nance, do you have a cuppa tea?"

"There's nothing in the larder. No milk."

"Come over to my place, then. My gent brought me a case of wine last night. Good stuff. We'll celebrate your arrival."

Lydia was happy to get away, and also curious to see another lightskirt's abode.

"You'd best lock the door and take the key," Sally said. "She keeps a spare there, just under the doormat." The doormat was inside the door. Lydia reached down and took up the key. Sally still didn't ask her how she had gotten in. Perhaps there was a man who took care of the building.

"Where is her maid?" Lydia asked, thinking this was another lead she could follow.

Sally laughed. "Did she tell you she had a maid? Sir John did get her one, but she said she'd rather have the extra blunt and sweep her own floors."

Sally's flat was not so very different from Prissie's place. It had the same sort of furnishings and decorations, but with woodcuts instead of watercolors on the wall, and a mirror in lieu of the series of tourist plates.

Sally poured them wine, a good claret, and they settled in to continue their chat.

"There's a do tonight at the Pantheon," she said. "The place where they have masquerade parties, you know. Why don't you come along?"

"You'll be going with your fellow, I suppose?"

"No, I'm meeting Warner there. He's going to a fancy dinner party at his wife's aunt's place first. She's a baroness," she said, lifting her nose in the air with her finger in jest.

"I don't have a domino."

"Prissie has one about somewhere. She won't mind you using it. You'll meet all sorts of fellows at the Pantheon."

"Will Dooley be there?" Lydia asked in a casual tone.

"Very likely. He's always hanging around, but you won't want nothing to do with the likes of him."

"I know Prissie doesn't like him much."

"Lord, she hates the sight of him."

"What did he do that she dislikes him so?"

" 'Twas some business they had going together when she first came to town and didn't know what he was like. She was with him for a while. I don't know exactly what it was, but he seems to think she owes him something. Money, I suppose. Your sister squeezes a penny pretty hard before she lets go of it. No offense I'm sure. It's all because of Richie. She's saving up to send him to a good school."

"Won't his papa help?"

Sally shrugged. "They don't like to hear about the outcome of their pleasure. It puts them off to mention kids. I know Prissie is footing Richie's bills herself. Mind you, Sir John's generous. A real gent. He'd like you, Nance. Where'd you learn to talk so fancy? Papa! Most of us call him Da or Pa. Must be that fine lady you was working for back home."

Lydia was glad to have her excuse handed to her. "That's it," she said, trying to tame her refined accent. "No harm sounding ton-ish."

"Some of them like it." Sally nodded. "More wine?" She held up the bottle.

Lydia's thoughts kept spinning back to Richie. It wasn't certain that her papa was the boy's father. If Richie was ten, then he might have been born just before her papa met Prissie. The father might be this Dooley. Sally held up her glass as if to make a toast, but before she spoke, the door knocker sounded.

"That'll be Warner," Sally said, and rushed to admit her patron.

Lydia didn't recognize the name, so she had no fear of being recognized. She heard a murmur in the hallway; then Sally said, "Sorry, sir, Prissie ain't at home, but her sister's here. You can have a word with her."

Lydia stared at the doorway, afraid she was about to be revealed as an impostor. She looked up to see Lord Beaumont staring at her in disbelief. His nostrils dilated, and his eyes glowed like hot coals.

"This here is Nancy Shepherd, Prissie's sister. This is Mr. Marchant, Nance. He has a message for your sister from her gent."

"How do you do, Mr. Marchant?" Lydia said, staring at him like a rabbit mesmerized by a snake.

"Miss Nancy," he said, walking forward and offering his hand. He drew her up from the sofa in a sudden, swift motion. "It will be better if we speak in private," he said to Sally. "You don't mind?"

"That's up to Nancy," Sally said with a belligerent air, looking from one to the other.

"That's fine, Sally," Lydia said. "We'll go to my sister's flat, Mr. Marchant."

"Come back when you're finished," Sally said, with a suspicious look at Beaumont. "We'll have lunch together, Nancy."

Beaumont ushered Lydia out the door, with a hand clamped firmly on her elbow.

Lydia's instinctive reaction was guilt, but by the time she got Prissie's door open, the guilt had turned to anger. She didn't have to account to Beaumont for her actions.

Chapter Eight

As soon as they were in Prissie's flat, Beaumont turned a fulminating eye on Lydia and flung her around to face him. "May I know what you think you're doing in that getup?" he demanded.

"I am endeavoring to discover who murdered Prissie Shepherd," she said, wrenching her arm free and striding into the parlor. He had to scurry after her to continue his tirade.

"We agreed that I would come to Maddox Street to make those enquiries."

"No, Beaumont, you agreed; you told me you would do it. I had nothing to say in the matter. I was to sit at home like a good little girl, twiddling my thumbs, until five o'clock in the afternoon, waiting for you to ride up on your white charger. You might as well realize right now that I intend to participate fully in this matter, with or without your so-called assistance."

"Did I wait until five o'clock to come here? I felt it would take me that long to complete my enquiries."

"Well, it did not take me that long. Of course, my enquiries did not involve any other activities," she said with a sharp look.

"What the devil is that supposed to mean?"

"Well, they are lightskirts, and you were awfully eager to meet them, without me along."

He shook his head in disgust. "You are your mother's daughter, Lydia. All men are lechers who can think of nothing but attacking women. Just what you hoped to accomplish by sneaking off—"

"I have already discovered a good deal—and without coming to harm. As to 'sneaking off,' you are not my keeper."

"Thank God for that! What do you think will happen if someone who knows Prissie's sister meets you? Say Dooley, for instance."

She tossed her chin in the air and began to stride the room, as she had often seen gentlemen do. "I'll handle that when and if it happens. I don't think he knows Nancy. He is some fellow Prissie met years ago when she first came to London."

"You'll handle it by posing as a lightskirt? Is that your idea of a sensible plan? You wouldn't fool a schoolboy with that accent. You don't look a bit like a lightskirt. Your gown is dowdy and your hair is all wrong."

"The gown, for your information, belongs to a lightskirt, Prissie. As to the hair, it fooled Sally, and she, you must own, would be as familiar with the breed as you are." She cast a furious glance at him. "Though of course from a somewhat different perspective."

Outdone on that angle, he tried a new attack. "You're wearing rouge! And have applied it very badly, I might add."

"What of it?" she said, and resumed her angry striding. Neither of them had sat down. "I am not posing as an experienced lady of pleasure, but as a girl fresh from the country looking out for a patron."

Beaumont tossed up his hands. "I don't believe what I'm hearing. You've gone mad. You were bad enough as a prude!"

Her gray eyes were frosty. "Thank you very much, Lord Beaumont. You were and are utterly hateful, thinking you know everything. I'll have you know I found out more in a quarter of an hour from Sally than you have accomplished since we got here."

"I just arrived this minute!"

"I mean here, in London. You had all yesterday afternoon and evening. All you found out was that Prissie's last name was Shepherd. I have found out all sorts of things. Horrible things," she said on a hiccoughing sob.

"What? What have you learned? Good God! Sir John didn't kill her!"

"Of course not! I don't mean that! I am convinced it was Dooley. Prissie was frightened of him. He said she owed him something—money, presumably. That's what he's been looking for here and at the inn."

"We already suspected that. What else did you learn?"

"Prissie has a son, a little boy. She calls him Richie. He's probably Papa's son, although his care is left entirely up to his mama. She let her maid go to save money for Richie's education."

"That ought to please you! You complained enough that your father was squandering money on her."

"It wasn't the money!" she said at once. "It was . . . oh, other things. He never came home for my birthday or Mama's. He let on he was too busy. He liked her better than us," she said, and drew a handkerchief from her reticule. She brushed away her tears and blew her nose.

"I'm sorry," he said, and felt a pronounced desire to punch Sir John in the nose. He and his mama had attended a few of those birthday parties. He remembered Lydia rushing to the window with love beaming in her eyes every time a carriage arrived, in the vain hope that her father had come home after all. And he remembered the slump of her shoulders when it wasn't Sir John, too. The light-skirt he could forgive, under the circumstances, but to ignore his own family was doing it too brown.

"She visits—visited Richie every Sunday," Lydia said, "and now she'll never visit him again. It's horrid! That poor little boy. And furthermore, you young gentlemen beat the lightskirts!" she said with a darkening eye. "And as soon as you see a prettier face, you jilt your mistresses. It is a shame and a disgrace what these poor girls have to put up with from you."

"I never beat a woman in my life."

"I wager you have jilted plenty!"

"You don't jilt a woman whose services you are buying. You give her her congé and a diamond bracelet, and often go to the trouble to find her a new patron as well."

"Trade her in on a new model, you mean, as if she were a carriage or a horse."

"She sells her wares to the highest bidder. It is not always the woman who is given her congé."

"Putting French words on it doesn't change anything. You use those women who have nothing to sell but their bodies! Oh, I am almost sorry I ever came here, except that I—" She came to a stop.

Perhaps she would not tell Beaumont about going to the Pantheon.

He leapt on it. "What?" he asked at once.

"Nothing. Just that I've learned all those things from Sally." She turned away and began fiddling with the ribbons on her gown, as she used to do when trying to con him a decade ago.

"You are a very bad liar, Lydia," he said, examining her in exasperation. Yet that childish motion with the ribbons, and her real hurt, caused him a wince of pity.

"So now it is a gentleman's prerogative to change his mind, is it? Yesterday you told me I was good at deceit."

Yesterday she had acted like a woman. Today, she was suddenly a young girl again. Beaumont sat down wearily and put his face in his hands. He must have been mad to come here. What did any of this have to do with him? He had thought it might be amusing to follow up the case, and now he was lumbered with a foolish, headstrong greenhead who was going to pitch herself and him into some calamity before it was over. Having brought her, he couldn't abandon her to a parcel of lightskirts and Dooley—whoever Dooley was. That was what she was hiding from him! She had a line on Dooley.

But she wouldn't tell him when she was in this temper. He'd take her home, and try to calm her down along the way.

"Come, I'll take you home now," he said gently.

Her chin squared in determination. "I am remaining in London for the time being. I am in no hurry to return to my lecherous father's house. The way I feel right now, I could not bear to look at him."

"I meant home to Grosvenor Square. Your father

86

is only human, Lydia, not the hero you imagined when you were a child. All men make mistakes—and all women, too. If you made him into a demigod in your mind, that is not his fault."

"I won't leave until I find out who killed Prissie. If he is mixed up in it, I want to see if I can at least keep him out of jail."

"That reason I can accept, and admire, but I doubt your mama will permit you to stay longer than another day."

"She'll let me stay as long as it takes. She thinks you are interested in marrying me," she said bluntly. "Don't blanch and tremble, Beaumont. If word gets about the parish and folks start to gossip, I shall jilt you and take all the blame of being a here-and-thereian."

His lips moved in silent amusement. "And who, pray, would believe it?"

She gave a derisive snort. "That I would jilt such an out-and-outer as Lord Beaumont? You have a good opinion of yourself."

"I meant that the redoubtable Miss Trevelyn would jilt anyone. You haven't a jilting bone in your body, my girl. A jilt moves more rhythmically. She sways, she undulates, she—"

"She sounds like a reed in the wind, moved by every zephyr."

"Just so, a reed swaying enticingly, and not a stiffly proud poplar, looking skyward."

"Is she also a thinking reed, as Monsieur Pascal mentions?"

"Ah no, thinking would be too much to ask of a mere woman," he said provocatively. "Thinking is confined to the male of the species. 'Man is a thinking reed,' you recall, is the quotation."

"If that was Pascal's meaning, then he is as bad as the rest of you. A pity man was not also a feeling reed, with some compassion for the less fortunate."

"He was French, you know," Beaumont said lightly, and regretted it at once. It was not an auspicious moment for levity. He could see that Lydia was truly upset. "I'll take you home now," he said again. "To Grosvenor Square, I mean."

"I can't go there yet. I told Aunt Nessie I was visiting a friend, Irene Coltrane, for lunch."

"Come to my place, then. We can discuss what other lines of enquiry we might make. Your papa might have left some notes or letters at his office at Whitehall."

She looked up, her eyes bright with interest. "Yes, that's possible. He wouldn't bring anything incriminating home to the Hall, and I found nothing in the town house except that one note. Very well. We'll do as you say."

Beaumont was not fooled into thinking she had changed her opinion of him. She had merely found another use for him.

"You said you would see Sally before leaving," he reminded her. "You had best do it before you change back to Miss Trevelyn."

"I'll go now," she said, and hastened out the door.

Sally was still in her apartment, polishing her nails. She jumped up when Lydia entered. "What did Mr. Marchant want you to tell Prissie?" she asked eagerly.

"Only that Sir John has gout, and won't be in town for a few more days."

"He's ever so handsome, Mr. Marchant. He looks well to grass. Why don't you throw your bonnet at him, Nancy? Ask him to take you to the Pantheon tonight."

"I'm going with you."

"We'll all go together. I'll meet my fellow there."

It was a sensible suggestion, but Lydia doubted that Beaumont would agree to taking her to such a raffish place.

"I believe he's busy tonight," she said, "but he's taking me out for a spin in his carriage now. What time shall we leave tonight?"

"Ten o'clock is plenty of time. It's not really lively before eleven. I'll call for you at ten."

"I'll be waiting."

"Good luck with Marchant."

Lydia returned to Prissie's flat to change back into her own gown. "I won't be a minute," she said to Beaumont, and went into the bedroom.

As soon as she closed the door, Beaumont went to call on Sally. After he had paid her a few compliments, he said, "Sir John is a little concerned about Prissie. Because of Dooley, you know," he said, as if he knew what he was talking about. "Has Dooley been troubling her?"

"He stops in from time to time, but with her out of town, there's nothing to worry about."

"After money, is he?"

"She never told me nothing, Mr. Marchant. You know how close she is about her own business."

"Would you know where I could get in touch with Dooley?"

"The likes of him don't advertise where they live, do they? Changes rooms every week to be safe from the law."

"He must have friends."

"His friends ain't my friends, nor Prissie's neither.

89

But if you're eager to see him, try the Pantheon tonight. After your other business, I mean. Nance mentioned you was busy. Me and Nancy are going."

Beaumont's triumph was heavily tinged with anger at Lydia's stunt of excluding him. "I might do that—but don't tell Nancy. I want to surprise her."

"Mum's the word."

When Lydia came out of the bedroom again dressed as herself, Beaumont was sitting at his ease on the sofa, leafing through a fashion magazine.

"All set?" he asked, rising and offering her his arm.

She ignored the arm and began to put on her bonnet. Beaumont put his hand under her chin and tilted her face up. She immediately stepped back.

"What do you think you're doing?" she demanded, hostility in every bone of her body.

He drew out his handkerchief and wiped the rouge from her cheeks. "Trying to make you look presentable," he said. "What did you think?"

She didn't answer, or have to. His glinting smile told her he had read her mind. She had thought he was going to kiss her. He returned the handkerchief to his pocket and walked to the door without waiting for her. Lydia stood a moment, recovering from her embarrassment, then hurried after him.

Chapter Nine

Beaumont now had two burrs under his saddle. It was bad enough that Lydia had accused him of foot-dragging; now she was making her own plans behind his back—and after he was kind enough to bring her to London. To show his eagerness, he said, "I'll take you to Manchester Square now and go on to Whitehall to see what I can discover there, before lunch."

"Why waste time?" His jaws clenched at the words, but she went on to explain. "I'll go to Whitehall with you and wait in the carriage, as I expect the Honorable Members would faint of shock to see a skirt in their hallowed halls."

"Very well, if you don't mind waiting. It shouldn't take long. Your papa's secretary knows we are neighbors, so I should have no difficulty getting into his office to retrieve a report on—something or other."

"The Corn Laws," she said. "He is always talking about them."

They drove directly to the Houses of Parliament and Lydia waited outside, as agreed. A colleague of her father's was just entering the House. Mr. Colville had been invited to Trevelyn Hall a few times in an effort to find a husband for Lydia.

Despite his handsome face and fine physique, she had not succumbed to his charms, perhaps because his visits had occurred in February, when she was in the throes of discovering her new philosophy. He recognized her at once and stopped a moment to talk.

"Miss Trevelyn! An unexpected pleasure. I didn't know you were in town, or I would have called. Is Sir John with you? We have missed him in the House."

"I fear he is still bedridden, Mr. Colville."

"I'm very sorry to hear it. Not serious, I hope?"

"Just his old complaint, gout. I'm visiting my aunt. I am just waiting for a neighbor, Lord Beaumont, who had to see to some business for Papa."

"I could have saved you the trip," he said, smiling in a strangely conspiratorial manner. "Sir John got the post. It was decided last night. He will be receiving official word today or tomorrow."

"What post are you speaking of?" she asked, thinking it would be yet another committee appointment. "He hasn't mentioned this."

Mr. Colville's eyes opened wide. "Did he not tell you the news? He wanted to keep it a secret, no doubt, until it was confirmed. He is being raised to the Cabinet for his excellent work these past years. A great honor!"

"The Cabinet!" she cried, almost in disbelief. This was astonishing news. It had been her father's dream forever. It would please him more than winning the state lottery, to be chosen as one of the elect to run the country. "How pleased he will be! Did he know of this pending promotion when he left?" she asked, wondering that her father would leave London at such a time, even if he had gout.

"He knew it was being discussed. He was as excited as a deb making her curtsey at court when he learned he was one of the three being considered. Lady Trevelyn will be happy to hear it. It might even prod her into removing to London."

"Thank you for telling me, Mr. Colville."

"My pleasure. May I have the honor of calling at Grosvenor Square?"

"I'm afraid I am making a very brief stay, and I have appointments both this afternoon and evening. But it was nice seeing you again. You must visit us soon at the Hall."

"I will be charmed, Miss Trevelyn." He tipped his hat and continued on his way.

Lydia sat, dumbfounded at what she had heard. Her papa to be a Cabinet Minister! From there, anything was possible, even the Prime Ministership. Sir John was still a young man, as politicians went. Why had he not told anyone? Even Nessie knew nothing about it. She could not have kept such exciting news to herself.

When Beaumont joined her, she was still in a daze, but she roused herself to attention and as the carriage lurched into motion, she asked if he had discovered anything.

"Nothing to do with Prissie, but I have a piece of news that should cheer you, and incidentally improve your opinion of your father."

"About the Cabinet post, you mean?"

"Oh, you knew," he said, disappointed to have the wind taken out of his sails. "Why the deuce didn't you tell me?"

"I didn't know. Papa never mentioned it. Is that not odd? Mr. Colville told me, just now."

"I see," Beaumont said, still disappointed, but at

least she had not been keeping another secret from him. "Yes, it is odd. What an unfortunate time for Sir John to be ill. He will not be here to accept the congratulations of his colleagues."

"The strange thing is, I don't believe he's ill at all," she said, frowning in perplexity. "He wouldn't let Mama call the doctor, and I have heard him walking up and down the hall when he is supposed to be in his bed."

"I would have thought it would take a dozen wild horses to keep him from the House these past few days. To push his promotion forward, you know. There is a deal of bargaining under the table in arranging these posts. You think his malingering has something to do with Prissie?"

"I don't know," she said in a confused voice.

Beaumont studied her a moment, noticing the shadow of fear and sorrow on her pale face. She might rail at men in general and her father in particular, but she wouldn't be so distraught if she didn't love him very much.

He took her fingers and gave them a squeeze. "It can't be that, Lydia," he said gently.

"What? What do you mean?"

"What you're thinking. That your papa lured Prissie out of town and killed her or had her killed. That he is mixed up in some way with whatever she and Dooley were involved in, and wanted to end it to avoid possible scandal at this time, when he is about to be honored."

She wrenched her hand from his. "I don't think that!" she said at once, but the two red splotches on her cheeks belied the hasty denial. "But you must own it looks suspicious," she added, peering to see what Beaumont thought. "Did you find nothing in his office? You were gone long enough."

"No, nothing. There was an interesting debate going on in the House. I listened in for a moment. Sorry I kept you waiting."

"Were they discussing Papa's appointment?"

"No, it had to do with counterfeit money. There is a new ring of smashers that has the Chancellor worried. It seems he got a bad bill himself. Eldon was delivering a fine rant." As they drew up to Beaumont's grand brick mansion on Manchester Square, he said, "What shall we do this afternoon? I shan't suggest a drive, though the day is fine. I know you don't want to waste any time enjoying yourself. You would rather be working on the mystery."

"I can't think of anything more to do at the moment," she admitted.

Lydia had visited Beaumont's London residence a few times in the past, on former visits to London. Her mama and Lady Beaumont were close friends. She had not been there for some years, however, and never alone with Beaumont. She still thought of the mansion as his papa's house, though the late Lord Beaumont had been dead for a decade. It was strange to think a young man like Beaumont owned all this.

Boots, the butler, rushed to the door to admit them. The place was much finer than her papa's house, as Pontneuf Chase was altogether grander than Trevelyn Hall. The gleaming brown marble floor and carved paneling should have been gloomy, but light streamed in from windows set high overhead to brighten it. A double archway showed a glimpse of the saloon beyond. It was not paneled but done in embossed plaster. Golden yellow window hangings, heavily pelmeted, gave the room a regal air yet did not overpower the senses. It was a livable room.

Beaumont handed his hat to the butler. "Two for lunch, Boots," he said. "Right away. A cold plate will be fine."

He led Lydia into the saloon to a striped sofa. He poured her a glass of wine. All this formal treatment made her feel very grown-up. The last time she had been here, she slid down the banister.

"I forgot how big this house is," she said, looking all around.

"Too big for one, certainly. I shall fill it with children one of these days."

"Do you have a—a special friend, Beau? I never thought to ask. That was thoughtless of me. There might be other things you want to do than help me."

"I have no one special in my eye. The Season was thin of beauties."

"And Miss Lawrence married a duke," she added mischievously.

"Just so. I and my broken heart are at your disposal. What shall we do this afternoon?"

His light answer told her he was over Miss Lawrence, if he had ever actually been in love with her. They were soon called to lunch, served in the morning parlor, as the party was so small. Over a light luncheon of cold viands and salad, they discussed what further steps they could take.

"If this Dooley man is a scofflaw, Bow Street might know his whereabouts," Beaumont suggested, hoping she would confide in him. He would attend the Pantheon in any case to keep an eye on her, but he thought it was time she trusted him.

"Why don't you go to Bow Street this afternoon and make enquiries?"

He studied her suspiciously. "Why don't we both go?"

"I want to think," she said in a weary voice. "About—all this. Papa and the lightskirts and the Cabinet post and—I don't know. It's very confusing. I daresay it is not all Papa's fault. I mean, Mama could have come to London with him so he would not be so much alone. And even at home—"

"Do they not get along?"

"He's hardly ever there. And when he is, Mama pays very little heed to him. I mean—she bustles about and tries to do everything to suit him, but—I don't know. She doesn't bother going to his room to say good night. Little things like that. I never really noticed before. She's dutiful, but not really friendly. And Papa is the same, really. They're more like . . ."

"Brother and sister?" he suggested, when she hesitated.

"No, not even that. Acquaintances, perhaps. But she would never look at any other man," she added in a defensive way.

Her revelation lured Beaumont into an admission. "My parents fought like cats and dogs," he said. "One hardly knows which is worse: a polite, conjugal indifference or an excess of emotion. The indifference would be easier on the crockery. Mama used to throw cups and plates at Papa."

"Really! What did they fight about?" she asked. She remembered Beaumont's papa as a jovial, handsome man, always laughing and joking. But then married people had two different faces, one for public and one for private. Now that she considered it, she realized her parents acted fonder of each other in company than when at home alone.

"Everything. Money, me, his friends, her friends, her bonnets and gowns, his horses and gambling. I don't know whether they hated or loved each other. Love, in the beginning, I daresay. Only a blighted love could lead to such rancor. Indifference wouldn't do it. 'Heaven has no rage like love to hatred turned,' as Congreve wrote. I always thought 'Hell has no rage' would be more like it."

"I don't think my parents ever loved each other. I can't remember ever seeing them snuggling or . . . you know. Making little private jokes and things, the way people in love do. But they never fought. They were always polite to each other. I wonder if Mama has known about Prissie all along."

"Or cared if she did know."

"That would be the saddest thing of all, wouldn't it?" she said, more to herself than to her companion. "To never have cared."

"Yet it's the course you've chosen, not to marry, not to care for a special someone."

She puzzled over this a moment. "I was speaking of people who do marry. In that case, they ought to love each other. For people like myself, it is quite different. We expend our emotions on different things." She thought of Nessie, who had surprised her by saying she regretted every day that she hadn't married.

"There speaks the voice of inexperience. When—if—you ever fall in love, you'll feel differently."

"Is that the voice of experience or merely the opinion of the omniscient male sex?" she asked with a rueful smile. Not the derisive smile she usually wore when quizzing him. It was softer, even vulnerable.

Beaumont just shook his head. "I'll say one thing, Lydia. If you ever do tumble into love, you won't do it blindly. You'll have a strong light trained on all the victim's faults. I never met such a mistrusting girl."

He thought she would flare up at him, but Lydia just laughed. She had enjoyed their little talk. It was interesting to hear the views of a young man-about-town.

"Victim! You make me sound like a harpy!"

"It's you who said it!"

"Then you're lucky I don't love you, for I would find faults aplenty. And before you jump down my throat, I admit you would find plenty in me."

"The redoubtable Miss Trevelyn admits to a fault?"

"Oh, certainly. I am my father's—parents' daughter, after all. I am ignorant as a swan, somewhat stubborn, I don't take kindly to orders, and I'm too skinny for the fashion."

"If that anticipatory smile suggests that you are now expecting a list of my faults, I am afraid you'll be disappointed."

The smile spread to a grin. "I already know your faults, Beau. What I was hoping for was a contradiction of mine. But then that would be expecting you to be gallant, which you are not. But I like you better than I did before."

"Before what?"

"Before we came here. It is kind of you to help me and Papa. I appreciate it."

"I shan't accept praise under false pretenses. I only came along for a lark."

She tossed her head in annoyance. "Don't ruin my compliment! You came, and you are sticking by me. And you aren't going to tell Aunt Nessie where I was this morning," she added, with a glance that was part question, part command, and part pure flirtation.

"Now I learn why the butter boat has been tipped in my direction!"

But to judge by his smile, he had no aversion to butter.

Chapter Ten

Lydia insisted on taking a hansom cab home, in case her aunt saw her alighting from Beaumont's carriage. "For I told her I was visiting Irene Coltrane," she explained. "Don't say it, I know! More deceit, but we do not want Nessie looking too closely into what we are doing."

Beaumont was concerned enough about her doings that he had his own carriage called and followed her to Grosvenor Square. He loitered around the corner for half an hour to make sure she didn't go out again. He found Lydia's behavior quite as mysterious as her father's. He knew as much about Sir John's affair with Prissie Shepherd as Lydia did, so what was she hiding from him? Why did she not want his help at the Pantheon? Had she discovered her father was involved in Prissie's death? If that was the case, then she was not only a loyal daughter but a courageous one.

While he pondered this, Lydia was busy devising a scheme to get away from her aunt to attend the masquerade party that night. When Nessie returned from her meeting with Lady Melbourne, she had heard of Sir John's promotion and was so excited, Lydia could have told her she was attending an orgy with Jack Ketch, and Nessie would hardly have noticed. Her brother's elevation to the Cabinet put her in the very top rank of political hostesses. It would call for larger parties, which would in turn call for a finer toilette. It would indirectly put more political patronage at her disposal, and in short give her as much influence in the social sphere as her brother would now have in politics.

When Lydia said, "I shall be going out this evening, Nessie. I will be taking a hansom cab to Manchester Square. Beaumont is having a few friends in after dinner," Nessie just smiled and nodded, and didn't even ask why she wasn't taking the family carriage.

"Beaumont will drive you home?" was her only question.

"Yes, of course."

"Excellent! Don't try to tell me there is not a romance brewing there!" This was more good news. She knew it was a match long hoped for at Trevelyn Hall. Nessie was in such a state of euphoria, she almost forgot to write to Sir John congratulating him. Of course, he would have been formally notified already, and would make plans to return to London, even if he had to come on a litter.

At nine-thirty, Lydia asked the butler to send a footman out to find a hansom for her. She drove directly to Maddox Street and admitted herself with the key she had taken that morning. It was eerie and frightening in the flat alone. Darkness had not fully settled in on this June evening, but the light was dim. Long shadows reached out at her from every corner. Strange, furtive sounds suggested someone lurking in their depths. She lit lamps in every room to lighten the gloom and looked around for any signs of intrusion. Everything was as she had left it.

She went into the bedchamber and searched the bulging clothespress for a domino. It was somewhat disconcerting to discover that Prissie's domino was a brilliant red. It made her feel like a scarlet woman. The mask that accompanied it was of black feathers with bugle beading around the edge. It was the kind that was held to the face on a wand, rather than attached by a band. When she was dressed with the mask covering her upper face, she lifted the domino hood over her head and went next door to call on Sally.

"What a turn you gave me!" Sally cried. "I could have sworn you was Prissie." Sally's domino was royal blue, with a matching mask. "Did you hear from Prissie?"

"No, nothing. How do we get to the party?" Lydia asked.

"Sometimes we walk. It's not far, just on Oxford Street, but tonight Joe will be dropping by for us. That's a fellow Mary knows—drives a hansom. He often stops here at night around this time to see if any of us girls want a drive anywheres. Mary's fellow plays the horses. She gives Joe tips. He made twenty quid last month. More than he makes on his hansom."

Lydia was glad she had a mask, for she felt extremely self-conscious loitering on the street corner with two lightskirts in the gathering darkness. They were so much a part of the scene in this neighborhood that they attracted little attention, none of it hostile. Any stray gentleman who passed lifted his hat and called, "Good night, girls," in a friendly way. Some of them offered a lift. The girls answered saucily.

"Does your ma know you're out alone?" the one called Mary shouted to a noble stripling who darted past in his curricle and whistled at them.

Lydia was relieved when the dilapidated hansom cab drew up beside them and the girls swarmed in. Mary, the most outspoken of the bunch, insisted on sitting on the bench with the driver and even took the reins, which she handled like a first-rate fiddler. By the time they reached the Pantheon, darkness had fallen.

Lydia had heard rumors of the Pantheon but had never been there or expected to be. She was surprised at the elegance of the place, when it had sunk into such disrepute that any lady who valued her good name dared not pass through its portals. It was a huge, sprawling building of fourteen rooms lavishly decorated in the Italian style. She goggled about at the somewhat faded grandeur of an enormous rotunda, a colonnade topped with a glazed dome, frescoes, stuccos, marble pillars, statuary, and glowing vases that held lamps inside.

After she had taken in the setting, she began to notice the noise and din and stench of wine and cheap perfume.

"We have a parlor abovestairs," Sally told her. The girls climbed the staircase to a private parlor that looked out on the ballroom, where the dancing was already in progress. At this early hour, it had not yet become very indecorous. Lydia studied the girls below with interest to discover how she ought to behave. She observed that they all walked with the same inviting wiggle to their hips and tossed their heads and hands about. They appeared to

104

have three modes of expression: pouting, smiling invitingly, and laughing more loudly than a lady would. It seemed a lightskirt was not allowed the luxury of frowning or scowling, if she wished to find or keep a patron.

Lydia leaned over to Sally and said, "Do you see Dooley here?"

"Not yet. You don't want to waste your time on the likes of him, Nance. There's Tommy Beerbaum. He's just given his girl her congé. Smile and he might come up."

A few gentlemen approached their table. As each of the girls except Lydia had a patron, they tried to direct the men's attention to their unattached colleague.

"Here's fresh goods, just up from the country," Mary said, tossing her head to Lydia, who blushed behind her mask and refused to dance with the dangerous-looking roué.

It was soon obvious that she would have no peace until she stood up with someone, so when a shy young gentleman called Bob invited her, she stood up with him.

Sally whispered in her ear as she left. "Wasting your time! He's still at university. Anyhow it's just as well you're with a gent, for there's Dooley."

Lydia gave a violent start. "Where?"

Nancy pointed to the ballroom below them. "The fellow in the dark green jacket. Leave it to Dooley not to bother with a masquerade costume. Unless he's masquerading as a gentleman. In that case, he ought to have hid his face."

He was easy to spot, as most of the men wore dominoes and masks. Lydia had been expecting some dark-visaged, oily, ugly man. She was surprised to see Dooley was handsome, or had been, once upon a time. A closer look showed the signs of dissipation around his eyes and mouth. He was tall and elegantly thin, about forty years of age, to judge by the silvering at his temples.

When she accompanied the man called Bob belowstairs, she strolled past Dooley, wiggling her hips and tossing her curls in the approved manner in hopes of gaining his interest. She succeeded, though it was Prissie's crimson domino and black mask that caught his attention. The musicians were taking a respite. The dancers stood around the floor in groups, talking, laughing, flirting. She noticed Dooley was watching her, and when she stood up to dance, she tossed an inviting smile at him over Bob's shoulder.

Bob was easy to handle. This trip to the Pantheon was his first foray into the demimonde. He was surprised at the ladylike manners of the lightskirt.

"I thought you girls would be . . . different," he said, smiling a question at her.

The remark brought Lydia to horrified attention. Her interest in meeting Dooley had put that aspect of the masquerade out of her mind. She must be more careful when she was with Dooley. She felt little doubt she would meet him soon. He seldom took his eyes from her.

She was unaware of the gentleman in the black domino and mask on the balcony, searching the ballroom of waltzers for her. He was one of a group, all similarly outfitted. Beaumont studied the room for a quarter of an hour; he even watched the woman in the scarlet domino with some interest, and still didn't recognize her. In frustration, he finally appealed to Sally.

"That's her in the red domino," Sally said, pointing below. "Why she ever bothered wasting her time with Bobbie Osgoode when Lord Haswell was after her I'll never know. I told her Bobbie was still a student."

Beaumont looked and gave a leap of recognition. Good God, the fair charmer was Lydia! And playing her role so well, he hadn't recognized her. When had that poker-backed girl learned to wiggle? And tossing her curls about like a female to the muslin born. A smile twitched his lips as he hurried below-stairs. The couple had joined the waltz by the time he reached them. Within thirty seconds, he was tapping Bobbie Osgoode on the shoulder.

"Sorry, old boy. This lady is taken. Miss Shepherd," he said, drawing her into his arms. She felt a little thrill of pleasure at this masterful gesture.

"Oh, I say!" Osgoode exclaimed, looking to Lydia for help.

"Sorry, Bobbie," she said, to avoid a ruckus. "I didn't think you would come to a place like this, Beaumont," she said as he spun her off. He couldn't see her upper face, but he noticed that her smile had dwindled to petulance. She didn't seem to be dancing with the same abandon as before either. Her movements were stiff.

"That shows how little you really know me. I, on the other hand, am not at all surprised that Miss Trevelyn, daughter of Sir John Trevelyn of Trevelyn Hall, is here, and on the very night of her papa's elevation to Cabinet Minister. Wouldn't the scandal sheets like to get hold of this!"

"You know perfectly well why I'm here!"

"What I don't know and greatly dislike is why you chose to keep it a secret from me. I thought we were working together. Are you keeping something from me, Lydia? Have you discovered something to Sir John's discredit—about Prissie's murder, I mean?"

Her gasp of shock told him this wasn't the reason for her secrecy. "Of course not!" she said.

"Then why did you sneak off here behind my back?"

She felt guilty about fooling him, and her guilt soon turned to anger. "I knew you wouldn't let me come!"

"Let you?" he asked. "I am not your papa. How could I prevent you? What I could and did do is come to protect you. Or young Osgoode, whoever required protection," he finished, scowling at her.

Lydia was much struck by his reply. That he could not stop her had never entered her head, despite the fact that he had no control over her. She realized she had become such a slave to the notion of male dominance that she hadn't even questioned it. Men made the rules and women obeyed, or if they disobeyed, they did it by chicanery.

"I thought you might tell Nessie," she said.

"As I told her about your trip to Maddox Street, you mean?" he asked, offended.

"Well, if that is how you feel, then I'm sorry, Beau. And I'm glad you've come, for I've found Dooley, and truth to tell, he looks a deal more dangerous than Osgoode. I would be happy if you would be nearby. And just how did you know I would be here?"

"That would be telling," he said, and laughed.

"You called on Sally this evening!"

"I did not, I promise you," he said with an easy conscience. He had paid his call on Sally in the morning.

"Well, in any case, you can't dance with me now;

Dooley has been casting leering looks at me and is just waiting for his chance to join me."

"Which one is he?"

"The rather handsome roué in the green jacket."

Beaumont felt a pronounced qualm when he saw the cut of Dooley's jib. The man had the undefinable air of one who lives by his wits, and doesn't much care who he hurts in the bargain. "He's too much for you to handle. I'll have a go at him."

"I don't think you're his type, Beau," she said, and walked away. He followed her off the floor.

"I doubt you are either. He won't be interested in a girl who holds herself like a poker."

Lydia looked back at him over her shoulder and resumed what she considered the walk of a lightskirt.

"Better," he murmured. "But your superior bit o' muslin don't wiggle. She sways."

She suddenly felt his hand on her hip, not lightly, but holding firmly. She turned and directed a cold stare at him. She knew she couldn't rant at him with Dooley watching, and his bold grin told her he knew it, too.

"Do it more slowly, Nance," he said, his fingers moving down over the swell of hips to her derrière. She was outraged at his daring to take such familiarity with her. "The same motion, but more slowly, with feeling. And smile. He's looking."

Her eyes glittered dangerously above her frozen smile. "If you don't get your hand off my bottom, Beaumont, I shall slap your face."

"Is it just my imagination, or are we beginning to sound like an old married couple?" he asked.

She continued swaying forward.

"There, that is much better," he said in a voice

suddenly husky. They reached the edge of the room and stopped. Lydia removed his hand and pinched it as hard as she could.

Beaumont chewed a grin. "Temper, temper, my pet. You are doing just fine for a tyro. I notice the chin is a centimeter lower as well," he said, looking down at her. "Now tilt it—just so." He caught it with his fingers and lifted her head. His dark eyes gazed into hers, which were sparkling with annoyance and something else—amusement, was it? For a long moment they simply stared at each other; then his head inclined slowly to hers. She waited until their lips were only an inch apart; then she stepped back.

"What do you think you're doing?" she asked. Her voice was breathless.

"Trying to convince Dooley of your assumed calling. Look around you."

A glance about the room showed her many couples were taking advantage of the dark corners to enjoy an embrace.

"I wouldn't want him to think I'm taken," she said, and walked away, leaving him standing alone feeling foolish. He watched as she swayed in Dooley's direction, and Dooley came forth, smiling like a tiger, to greet her. Without speaking, he put out his hand, and she accepted it.

"I don't believe I've had the pleasure," he said, lifting a black eyebrow in question.

Lydia looked into a pair of diamond-hard eyes, world-weary and dissipated. She did not think this man would be infatuated with an inexperienced greenhorn, fresh from the provinces. A more sophisticated sort of lightskirt would appeal to him.

"What makes you think you will have it now, sir?" she asked with a cool look.

110

"I have at least the pleasure of looking."

"A cat may look at a queen," she riposted, and walked on.

Dooley walked a pace behind her. "You didn't turn him off for no reason," he said. "Come, my pretty. I have champagne waiting at my table just for you."

"Do you read minds, then, that you knew I'd be here?"

"That's it," he said, and placing her hand under his elbow, he piloted her abovestairs to a private box.

Beaumont watched with a sinking heart. Then he hurried after them.

Chapter Eleven

The champagne was brought to the box and Dooley poured two glasses. He touched his glass to hers and said, "To the future."

"I'll drink to that," Lydia said, adopting a common accent. "What's your name, then, mister?"

"First, my dear, what is yours?"

"You can call me Nancy."

"Put down your mask, Nancy, and let me see your lovely face." He didn't wait for her to do it, but reached out and took the mask from her.

He studied her for a long moment, his dark eyes darting over her hair, her eyes, nose, and mouth. "You don't look much like your sister," he said.

"Who says I have a sister, and what is it to you?" she asked pertly.

"This mask says it," he replied, running long, artistic fingers over the gleaming feathers. "I bought it for Prissie some years ago."

"Then you'd be Dooley. I've heard my sister mention the name," she said, but gave no idea what she may have heard of him, other than that he had given Prissie the mask.

"Priss and I were bosom bows," he said. He kept watching her intently as they talked. "Where is she, Nancy? I thought she'd be here."

Lydia allowed a frown to seize her brow. "I don't know. I wrote and told her I was coming. She didn't answer, so I came ahead. But when I got here, there wasn't a sign of her. Sally thinks she's off visiting her lad."

"You're staying at her place?"

"Just till I get rooms of my own."

"Any special reason why you came at this time?"

"My ma figured it was time I started earning my living," she said vaguely.

"How do you plan to do that? Following the family profession, are you?"

"What do you think?" she asked with a shrug.

"I think that with that face, you should do well." He lifted his glass to her. "Here's to your success. I might put you in the way of a well-inlaid gent."

She gave a dismissive laugh. "I'm not sure I'll need your help, thankee all the same."

They drank a moment; then Dooley said, "Has Prissie sent anything home to her ma lately? Just before you left, it would be."

Lydia came to attention. This suggested it was Dooley who had searched Prissie's flat—and her room at the inn in Kesterly. It seemed he had not found what he was looking for, since he asked this question. "She sent some muslin," she replied with a smile that suggested she knew more than she did.

"Nothing else? A smallish package it would be, heavy."

They exchanged a long, measuring look. Lydia had an instinctive feeling Dooley would lose interest in her if he felt she didn't know what he was talking about. A smallish, heavy something. What could it be?

"No, she didn't," she said. "Would she have taken the package with her when she went to see Richie?"

"Nay, I've already been to the Nevils'. I smashed that ken and a few other spots. They weren't there."

"I noticed you'd searched her flat as well," she said, smiling knowingly. *They* weren't there. At least she could stop calling the items "the package."

"No grass growing under your feet."

"Would she have given them to her fellow, Sir John?'"

"I doubt she'd do that. He didn't know what she was at, did he?" Lydia breathed a sigh of relief. Whatever "they" were, her papa was not mixed up in it. "Him a big shot in the government. He's the last one she'd give them to."

"That's true," she said. This suggested the "them" was something illegal. "Did you talk to Sally at all?"

"I know for a fact Prissie never told Sally about it. She didn't tell any of her friends. Just me and Prissie—and you—are the only ones as know."

"And we won't tell," Lydia said playfully.

Dooley didn't smile. "Not if we know what's good for us. Let's get away from here and go somewhere we can talk business, Nancy," he suggested. As the evening went on, the place became rowdier and noisier.

Lydia was delighted with the progress she was making with Dooley, yet she didn't want to leave the safety of the crowded Pantheon with him to go to some isolated spot.

"I was with a gent," she prevaricated. "He was going to take me out for a spin in his rig."

"Tell him you've made other plans. I'll make it worth your while."

Lydia considered his offer. She felt she really

must go with Dooley, but not entirely alone. She'd tell Beaumont, and he could follow them.

"All right. Just give me back my mask," she said.

Dooley handed her the mask. She lifted it to hide her face and went to look for Beaumont. He was loitering outside Dooley's box.

"Did you hear what he was saying?" she asked.

"I did, and you're not going anywhere alone with that hedgebird."

"But he's practically told me everything! I have only to learn what's in the package and we shall discover who killed Prissie, and prove Papa had nothing to do with it. I am convinced Dooley is behind it all."

"Of course he is. He's killed Prissie, and he'll kill you as well when he learns you can't help him."

She hesitated as this ominous possibility struck home, then firmed her resolve. "That's why you must follow us. I'll invite him back to Prissie's place. He only wants a quiet place to talk. I'll leave the door unlocked when we go in. If you hear me scream, come in and rescue me."

Beaumont felt a lurch of fear for her. "We know Dooley's our man. You don't have to go with him. I'll follow him, keep an eye on him."

"He wouldn't be as forthcoming with you as he is with Prissie's sister. I must go, Beau. You can see that."

He could see it, but he didn't like it. He was coming to know Lydia well enough to realize she would go, with or without him. "Very well, but for God's sake, be careful, Lydia. Dooley's a dangerous man."

"I am perfectly aware of it. I only wish I had a pistol."

"I have one in my carriage. I'll bring it along."

"Thank you, Beau. What an excellent friend you are." In her excitement and gratitude, she reached up and placed a kiss on his cheek before running back to Dooley. Beaumont stood scowling, wondering how he had gotten himself into this ridiculous position. If anything happened to her, he would be responsible. How could he explain it to Sir John and her mama if anything happened to her? How could he live with himself? He shouldn't let her go, and he couldn't stop her.

He hurried belowstairs and called for his carriage. Before it arrived, Dooley and Lydia came down and went out the front door. Dooley didn't have a carriage. Beaumont overhead him say, "We'll stroll along until we meet a hansom."

They turned toward Maddox Street. He kept them in sight until his own carriage arrived, then followed slowly behind, taking care not to overtake them. When Dooley hailed a hansom, Beaumont followed behind it, wary lest it take a turn away from Prissie's flat. It drove directly there, however, and stopped. Dooley helped Lydia from the rig, like a gentleman. Beaumont drove past, then drew his pistol from the side pocket, pulled the check string, and got out of his carriage.

"Drive on. Keep circling the block until I come out," he said to his coachman.

As the carriage drove off, he stood in the street, wondering where he should post himself to protect Lydia. He wouldn't be able to see or hear the parlor if he waited outside the kitchen window, which would give him easy access to the flat and concealment from the street. If he waited in the foyer outside Prissie's parlor, Dooley would see him when

116

he left. But that was the best spot to be if Lydia needed help. He strode into the house. The foyer was empty. He went on tiptoe to Prissie's door and listened.

In the little parlor, Lydia perched nervously on the edge of a chair and Dooley took up the sofa opposite.

"What did you have in mind, then?" she asked bluntly.

Dooley sat, his dark brow furrowed. "I'm in a bit of a spot, Nancy. Prissie got some bee in her bonnet and ran off with what didn't belong to her. I paid her a thousand pounds for her work and got nothing for my trouble. The wench said she deserved a bigger cut. She took the money and ran out on me. I don't believe she took them with her. I've searched every place she's been. I know she had them here last week. I saw them, and they were mighty good. Said she just wanted to do a little fine-tuning."

"Can't you wait till she comes back?"

"Who says she's coming back?" She stared into his hard eyes. She could almost feel the evil emanate from him. She was sure he had killed Prissie—and he would kill her, too, if it suited him. She didn't trust herself to speak.

Dooley continued, "Wilkie and the boys are eager to get started. The distribution's all set. We've been working on it for a year. You chat around to her pals. She must have given them to someone for safe-keeping. They'll hand them over to her sister. Find the plates, and there's a thousand pounds in it for you. Have we got a bargain?"

Lydia considered it a moment. She was eager to agree and be rid of Dooley, but she felt Prissie's sister would drive a harder bargain.

"Make it fifteen hundred and you've got a deal."

"Done!" He reached out and shook her hand.

"Where can I reach you if I find them?"

"I'll be in touch with you."

He rose and she accompanied him to the front door. "Here's a little something to tide you over," he said, and stuffed a wad of crumpled bills into her fingers. "Don't spend it all in one place, as the saying goes. Good advice in this case. I'm glad to see you're a sensible gel, Nancy. I think me and you could get along just fine."

Lydia's instinct was to throw the money in his face, but she knew she had to play her role to the end. She snatched at the bills eagerly, with a quick glance to see their denomination.

"How's about a little kiss before I go?" he asked, putting one arm around her waist.

She felt soiled to touch him. "Let's not mix business with pleasure, Dooley."

"It never stopped your sister."

"I ain't my sister," she said, pushing him off. He reached for her again.

Beaumont, still listening in the hall, had heard their footsteps approach the door. He'd intended to dart up the stairs when he heard Dooley leaving, but curiosity got the better of him. He could hear their voices within and some of their words. When he heard the conversation stop and scuffling sounds begin, he was afraid Lydia had run into trouble. He was glad to be there when it happened, and hoped it would cure her of this harebrained notion of pretending to be Prissie's sister. After one sharp rap on the door, he strode in and directed a menacing stare at Dooley.

Dooley took one look at Beaumont's angry face

and shook his head at Lydia. "Crikey, you don't waste much time," he said, and strode out.

Beaumont slammed the door behind him, then turned his fulminating eyes on Lydia. "I hope you've learned your lesson! I heard that noise. Did he attack you?" Without waiting for an answer, he turned to follow Dooley. "I'll darken his daylights."

"Don't be so . . . masculine, Beau," she said, laughing at him. "That sound you heard was not me fighting for my virtue, but only the dance of negotiations."

"Was he offering you money?" he demanded.

"Yes."

"Propositioning you, in other words!"

She smiled demurely. "In a way, I suppose he was."

"I hope you put the hedgebird in his place."

"It would have looked very odd if I had refused."

"You mean you accepted money from him! Lydia, this is intolerable."

She held up the wad of bills. "But such a lot of money! Fives and tens. It's—it's over fifty pounds, Beau. And I didn't even let him kiss me." She scowled at him. "Just how much does it cost you men to hire a woman, I should like to know."

For quite thirty seconds he was beyond words. When he spoke, it was a command. "Change your clothes. I'm taking you home."

"Don't you want to hear what I learned? I am practically working with Dooley. He's going to pay me fifteen hundred pounds."

Beaumont was so incensed, he didn't trust himself to speak. He took Lydia by the shoulders and marched her to the door of Prissie's bedroom.

"Change, now. We'll talk on the way home. I want to get you out of here in case he comes back."

119

"He won't. Not tonight. He thinks you're my fellow."

She laughed and flung the fistful of bills into the air, then went into the bedroom and closed the door.

Chapter Twelve

Lydia came out of the bedroom a moment later wearing her own mantle, but the rouge was still on her cheeks and her hair was in an unaccustomed tousle of curls. She saw the money was still on the floor.

"We can't leave this here," she said, and began picking it up to stuff in her reticule. "I shall give it to Nessie for her orphans."

Beaumont had managed to get his temper under control. "Well, what did you learn from Dooley?" he asked.

"Plates," she said. "Prissie made some plates for him. He paid her a thousand pounds for them, but she demanded more, and when he refused to pay, she ran off with them."

"Plates?" Beaumont asked, blinking in confusion. "Why would he pay so much for plates?"

"I don't know. They must have been very special plates. Prissie does collect plates," she said, glancing at the wall that held a motley arrangement of them.

They both went to examine the collection of tawdry plates for some hidden value. "If any of these are worth more than a shilling, I would be surprised," he said, reading the inscriptions. "Tunbridge Wells, home of the famous Chalybeate Springs." In the center of the plate, a shield held a picture of the Parade, with its row of lime trees. Another was of "Weymouth, the Royal Resort." Beneath the inscription was a likeness of Gloucester House, where George III used to holiday before he ran mad.

"It can't be this sort of plate," Lydia said. "The ones Dooley spoke of were small. And heavy. I have been thinking about it. They must have been a forgery of some valuable historical memorial plates. The originals were probably in gold. I expect they've forged some in pinchbeck to sell to unwary victims."

"Prissie painted. She didn't work with metal. It would require a smelting works or some such thing to make gold plates."

"He said plates."

Beaumont stood a moment, brooding. "You must have misunderstood him. Perhaps it was rates, or gates, or—or weights," he said, flinging out his hands.

"I am not deaf, Beau. He said plates. Furthermore, he would not pay her a thousand pounds for weights, and one could hardly wrap up a set of gates in a small parcel."

Beaumont spotted one of the bills on the floor and reached to pick it up. He looked at it, frowning. "Let me see the other bills," he said. She fished them out of her reticule and handed them to him. A slow grin spread across Beaumont's face. "Plates," he said, and laughed. "Of course. Plates."

"What? What is it?"

"She made plates for forged banknotes."

"Forged? You mean Dooley gave me counterfeit money?"

"It seems a suitable payment. Counterfeit money for counterfeit love. The serial numbers are all the

122

same on the fives." He checked the tens. "Yes, on these as well. I wonder if this is from the lot Eldon was complaining of in the House this morning. That would explain why Dooley is eager to get new plates—probably for different denominations."

"Oh! That is why he said not to spend it all in one place. And that is what he meant by the distribution! He said the distribution was all set. How clever of Prissie! I wonder how she learned to do it."

"She had some skill as a forger, or so I assumed from the Dürer prints. It would be more difficult to work on the copper plates, but not impossible."

"Then she quarreled with Dooley and ran off with the plates. The question is, what did she do with them?"

"I doubt she left them behind when she went to Kesterly," Beaumont said. "She would know Dooley would be looking for them."

"He searched every place she had been. The Nevils', where she kept Richie, the inn at Kesterly, as well as her flat here. Where would she have put them for safekeeping, I wonder?"

They stood a moment, looking at the forged bills. One possible answer occurred to them both at once. "You don't think—" Lydia said, as Beaumont exclaimed, "Sir John!"

"But she would never tell Papa what she was doing."

"She wouldn't have to. She might have asked him to hold on to a parcel for her. A smallish, heavy parcel."

"If she gave it to him, it is at Grosvenor Square. He would never take anything belonging to her to the Hall."

They extinguished the lamps, locked the door, and

went out into the street, where Beaumont's carriage was just turning the corner. "Do you see any sign of Dooley?" Beaumont asked, looking around.

"No, and even if he sees us, he'll just think I've accepted your patronage," Lydia said unconcernedly.

Beaumont looked at her and shook his head. Lydia Trevelyn was not the prude he had taken her for. In the carriage, she turned to him, grabbed his arm, and gasped.

"Beau! I've just thought of something! There is a smallish, heavy parcel in Papa's office! I saw it on his desk. I even picked it up, but it was too heavy to contain billets-doux, so I didn't pay any heed to it. What shall we do with the plates? Should we turn them over to Bow Street? Prissie is already dead, so they cannot hang her."

"They would be interested to learn what Sir John was doing with them."

"We'd have to do it anonymously. That would fix Dooley's wagon!"

"It wouldn't help Prissie, and it wouldn't put Dooley behind bars either. I think we should use the plates to catch him."

"I do feel sorry for Prissie, but avenging her death is not my top priority. I have to think of Papa. She was not only a lightskirt and a criminal, she used Papa to hide behind. Imagine if the plates were found in his house. He'd be ruined. We should just throw the plates down a well. That would be the least troublesome way to be rid of them."

When the carriage reached Grosvenor Square, they went into the house. "Is my aunt home yet?" Lydia asked the butler.

"Not yet, Miss Trevelyn. It's only eleven-thirty. She is usually out a little later than this."

"Thank you, Blake. Would you make us some tea, please?" she said, to be rid of him.

As soon as he was gone, she rushed into her father's office. The smallish parcel sat on the edge of the desk. She snatched it up and began pulling at the strings. Inside was a small box of heavy cardboard. Her breath came in short pants as she lifted the lid. She looked at the contents, blinked, and looked at Beaumont.

"Well?" he asked, stepping forward to see for himself.

"It's a clock," she said.

Beaumont took the box, removed the clock, and began to examine it.

"The plates aren't inside it, Beau. It's the little French boudoir clock from Mama's bedchamber. It stopped running a month ago. Papa brought it to London to have it repaired. He either forgot to take it home or it has come since he left. What a take-in."

She gave a weary sigh, her shoulders sagging. She looked ready to bawl.

Beaumont felt a rush of some tender emotion. "That's not to say the plates aren't here somewhere in the house," he said bracingly.

"That's true!" she said, brightening. "And the likeliest place for them to be is either here or in his bedroom. We'll look here first."

They began pulling out drawers, opening cabinet doors, and peering under the bed. It didn't take them long to learn the parcel was not in the study.

"His bedchamber," Lydia said, and headed for the door.

They met Blake, just carrying the tea tray into the saloon. Lydia just glanced at it. "Oh, you have brought plum cake. How nice, but do you know,

Blake, Beaumont was just saying he would like some bread and butter and cold mutton. Would you mind terribly?"

Blake bowed his obedience, set the tray on a table, and left. They immediately ran upstairs to Sir John's bedroom. It was more difficult to search. Besides the toilet table, the desk, the bed, and the clothespress, there was the sitting room, with countless places to hide a small box. By the time they returned belowstairs, breathing hard and empty-handed, the second tray had been delivered.

"I don't know what Blake must think," Lydia said, and gave a nervous laugh.

As the words left her mouth, the butler appeared at the archway. "Will there be anything else, Miss Trevelyn?" he asked politely, but his darting eyes took in her breathless state and her toilette, which had become mussed from her frantic search. He frowned heavily at her escort.

"That will be all, thank you," she said primly, but with a laughing eye at Beaumont.

"He thinks we've been carrying on," Beaumont said. "We had best be careful, or Sir John will be demanding to know my intentions."

"I've already promised I would jilt you, if worse came to worst."

"It is not very flattering to hear myself spoken of as the worst," he said, picking up a sandwich while Lydia poured the tea. He watched with interest as she daintily poured, with her white wrist gracefully curved in the approved fashion. It seemed homey, the two of them having tea together.

She gave him a saucy smile. "I wager you receive enough flattery from the ladies. It will do you good to realize not everyone would jump at an offer."

"Of course not every one. Just most of them," he riposted. "Some misguided ladies have taken the unaccountable notion they want to be spinsters."

"You or no one, eh? Such conceit," she said, taking up another sandwich.

She glanced across the room to a silver cigar humidor on a side table. It was about twelve inches long, nine wide, and six deep. She rose and went to lift the lid. Beaumont watched. He noticed she didn't walk as stiffly as she had before. Not so wiggly as when she was being Nancy, but there was a noticeable difference. She was more relaxed, more womanly, more interesting. . . .

The humidor held half a dozen cigars, but no plates. She looked around the room and began to consider other spots. A pair of large China vases sat on either side of the fireplace. She peered in. Seeing what she was doing, Beaumont rose and looked in a bombe-fronted chest in a corner and other possible spots.

In one dark corner stood a high Queen Anne cabinet holding a selection of small china Limoges ornaments. Lydia dragged a chair to it and climbed up to peer on top of the cabinet. "Let me do that," Beaumont said, when he saw what she was doing.

The movement of the chair and their talking diverted them from hearing the front door open.

"Don't bother. There's nothing here but dust," she said, wiping her hands.

Beaumont lifted his arms to assist her from the chair and she placed her hands on his shoulders. Her waist felt small and warm beneath his fingers. He lifted her bodily from the chair, while her skirts swung about her ankles. When he placed her on her feet, he kept his hands about her waist as he gazed down at her, and she looked up at him with a question in her eyes. The air seemed hushed as they continued looking. They were in this peculiar position when Nessie entered the saloon.

"Good gracious! What are you doing, Lydia?" she asked.

"Beau was just helping me down from the chair," Lydia said, pointing to the chair and blushing like a peony. "I was looking for a ball on the top of that cupboard."

"What would a ball be doing up there?"

"Beau threw it up. Oh, years and years ago," she added, as she had no ball to produce. "We were just talking about the old days. You remember my birthday party, here in London some years ago. Beau and his mama came. He thought he was much too mature for such childish goings-on and threw the ball up there for an excuse not to play with me." She stopped then, as she realized she was rambling.

Nessie was happy to hear the young couple were reliving their youth. She peered at Lydia and said, "My dear, is that rouge I see on your cheeks? And what on earth have you done to your hair?"

Lydia's inventiveness failed, and Beaumont stepped in to rescue her.

"Did Lydia not mention my little impromptu party this evening was a masquerade?" he said.

"No, she didn't. What did you go as, Lydia—a lightskirt?" Nessie laughed merrily.

Beaumont and Lydia exchanged a quick glance and bit back their laughter. "An actress," Lydia said. "We just wore dominoes. It wasn't a very elaborate party."

"You got home early."

128

"I'm afraid it was a very boring do," Beaumont said. "And how was your evening, Miss Trevelyn?"

"Marvelous. I do wish John had been there. Everyone was asking about him, and sending their congratulations. Lady Jersey was hinting that Almack's could use another hostess. Imagine!"

"Quite an honor," Beaumont said, feigning enthusiasm for this dullest of the dull social clubs, which maintained its aura of exclusivity. Princes and generals were spurned if they did not adhere to the club's strict standards of dress and deportment.

Sensing that she had interrupted an intimate moment, Nessie said, "You had best say good night to Beaumont now, dear," and left them to make their farewells in privacy.

"Your talent for deceit is slipping," Beaumont said, when they were alone. "Who would play ball in a saloon?"

"You would."

"It wasn't a ball. It was just a piece of paper I squeezed up when you insisted on playing some childish game."

"Now I remember! It was tic-tac-toe. And you only squeezed up the paper because I was beating you. And you didn't bring me a present either." She gave a sniff of offense at this ancient slight.

"I didn't know it was your birthday! Mama dragged me along."

"You always knew my birthday was the ninth of May," she said with a pout.

When she realized she was behaving childishly, she blushed, then tried to hide it with a scowl. "You had best go. Nessie will be waiting to hear me come up."

"That is one of the scourges of being a spinster,"

he said nonchalantly, but he peered to see if the warning had hit home.

Annoyed by this reminder, she took his arm and propelled him into the hall. "Blake will see you out. Good night, Beaumont. Thank you for the very boring masquerade party."

"You are entirely welcome, Miss Trevelyn. Would you care to accompany me on a very boring drive tomorrow afternoon?"

"Won't I see you in the morning?" she asked.

"Such eagerness! I am flattered. At this rate, worse may come to worst sooner than I fear—thought."

He picked up his curled beaver, put it on at a jaunty angle, and left, smiling.

Chapter Thirteen

Lydia found, after she was in bed, that she was not in the least tired despite her busy day. She had experienced such a confusion of new thoughts and met people so different from her usual friends that she felt her life had turned upside down. She had finally met a group of women who were free of the usual social strictures, only to discover they were still ruled by men and were immeasurably worse off than herself.

How childish her complaint seemed when placed beside the hardships of girls like Sally and Mary and even Prissie Shepherd, whom she had never met, but felt she was coming to know indirectly. When she thought of Prissie taking such risks to provide a good home for her son, she felt she had misjudged the woman. What had she meant to Papa? What had he meant to her?

It seemed impossible that she could have loved a man old enough to be her father. No, he had been a necessary evil, the best of a bad lot. The older gents were nicer to you, Sally had said, but making them happy was a job, not a pleasure. It sounded a perfectly wretched life. No wonder Prissie had turned to helping Dooley with his counterfeiting scheme. It would free her from her other profession and provide a good nest egg for her son.

The greatest trial of her own pampered life was that kind, well-meaning gentlemen wanted to wrap her in cotton wool. It was frustrating, but compared to putting up with the vagaries of a man who cared for nothing but his own enjoyment, her life was one of ease and luxury. And when the gentleman tired of his girl, he left her. If she happened to be lumbered with his child, that was her lookout. They didn't want to hear about the consequences of their selfishness. Of course, not all gentlemen were so hard-hearted. No doubt some of them truly cared for their mistresses and treated them not only well but lavishly.

She could not forget her papa's indiscretion, but she was perilously close to understanding his position, and to understand is to begin to forgive. It must have been lonely for him in London, away from his family. After a hard day's work, naturally he would want some relaxation and easy female companionship. It was no new thing for a man to stray from the vows of matrimony, and at least he had been at pains to protect his family. He had chosen a modest mistress and apparently treated her well, except in the matter of Richie.

If she ever married—not that she necessarily would—she would behave quite differently from her mama. She would go where her husband went and watch out for his welfare. If only her mama were more like Nessie, all would have been well at home. Nessie was the kind of wife a politician needed. A wife need not devote all her time to house and home and embroidery. Her husband ought to be her major concern.

Nessie and Mama—each had only half a life. Nessie lived on the edge of her brother's life, picking up the crumbs of his success. She had nothing but her social life and the charity work that was almost a part of it. She had missed out on the satisfaction of a husband and family, a home of her own. Nessie's major achievement, if she did achieve it, would be to reign as one of the hostesses at Almack's. She had her charity work, but Lydia was no longer convinced that would be enough to fill her own life. If she married someone like Beau, who was not so managing as most gentlemen, marriage might be tolerable.

Then her mind turned to the more immediate puzzle of finding the plates and discovering who had murdered Prissie. Dooley, of course, was the obvious suspect. He had followed her to Kesterly. When he saw her heading to Trevelyn Hall, had he feared she was going to reveal her guilty secret to Sir John and ask his help? He realized Sir John was a man of power and influence. Had Dooley killed her, thinking he would find the plates in her reticule or in her hotel room? But Prissie had outwitted him. Where had she hidden them? Perhaps Papa had put them in the attic. She would search it first thing in the morning.

It was late when she finally fell asleep, and late the next morning when she awoke. A glance at the clock told her it was nine o'clock. The golden shafts seeping into her room from the edge of her window blind promised a sunny day. As she rang for tea and a maid to help her prepare her toilette, she thought with a pang of Prissie and Sally and all their sisterhood, living hand to mouth in a small flat, with no servants.

133

As the day was fine, she dressed in her pink-sprigged muslin with the green sash. Even before going belowstairs for breakfast, she went up to the attic. Four large rooms, half full of trunks and discarded lumber, suggested it would be a daunting task to find one small parcel concealed there. She would have breakfast first, and speak to the butler. The parcel might have arrived after Papa left. Blake would have put it away, possibly in his own room. When she went below, she asked Blake if a parcel had come for her father within the last week.

"It's Lady Trevelyn's French clock you're thinking of. It arrived two days ago. I put it in Sir John's study, Miss Trevelyn."

"Did any other small parcels arrive?" she persisted.

"No, miss. I'll let you know at once if it comes. A birthday present for Master Tom, is it?" he asked. Blake had been with the Trevelyns forever and felt quite one of the family. He knew her brother's birthday was looming at the end of the month.

She nodded and said, "Very likely he asked to have the parcel sent to the Hall," to quell his curiosity.

"That would be it. Sir John is always very thoughtful of his family, despite his heavy load of work."

Nessie had arisen early and was busy with her correspondence in the small parlor set aside for her private use. She came out when she heard Lydia.

"Such a load of cards have arrived, congratulating your papa," she said happily. "And dozens of invitations. I wonder when he will be arriving. I must answer these, but cannot like to refuse an invitation to Carlton House. I'm sure John will arrive today. He would have written if he could not come."

Lydia also felt her papa would soon be landing in on her, and with this in mind, she made a quick search of the rest of the house in case Prissie had given him the parcel in person, thus avoiding Blake's sharp eye. She was in the attic, delving into trunks of old clothes packed in camphor, when a maid came up to find her.

"Sir John has just arrived, Miss Trevelyn," she said, all smiles. "He has been asking for you. I know you would want to congratulate him."

"Oh, indeed. Thank you, Mary. I'll be down as soon as I wash my hands."

Sir John was in Nessie's parlor, discussing the correspondence with her. Lydia stood a moment, looking at him. He wore a triumphant smile as Nessie mentioned her various social conquests. When he saw Lydia, he looked up and held out his arms. All her old anger resurfaced when she saw him, wreathed in glory, with never a thought to poor Prissie.

She didn't fly into his arms, but just said, "Congratulations, Papa," in a cool voice.

"Is that all you have to say?" he asked, hurt at her obvious reluctance to go near him.

"I do have something I would like to say in private, Papa, if you will excuse us, Nessie."

"Not a lovers' spat, I hope!" Nessie said. "You and Beaumont have been getting on so well, I quite expected to see him for breakfast. Don't keep your papa long, Lydia. I have a hundred matters to discuss with him."

"This won't take long," Lydia said, watching as her father's smile dwindled to a frown. She noticed that he was looking hagged, with circles under his eyes and a drawn look about the mouth.

Nessie, always the soul of discretion, closed the door behind her as she left.

Sir John cast a wary eye on his daughter. "What is it, Lydia?"

There seemed no subtle way to ask what she had to ask. "I want to know about your mistress, Prissie Shepherd, Papa," she said bluntly.

His color faded, and his eyes opened wide. "Prissie Shepherd! How did you— Where—"

"You know she's been murdered? She was the woman found in the river at home."

He slumped onto a chair, his shoulders sagging, and shaded his eyes with his fingers. "Yes, I learned of it yesterday," he said in a shaken voice. "Your mama kept it from me. She didn't know of my relationship with Prissie. She just didn't want to upset me, because of it happening so close to home. Horace Findley called to congratulate me on this appointment. He told me they had identified the girl in the river as Prissie. They found her reticule under her bed at the inn."

Lydia remembered then that she and Beau hadn't looked under the bed. Dooley must have put it there.

"You knew about the counterfeit plates?" she asked.

He removed his hand and looked at her in confusion. "What is this? She told me she had got rid of those Dürer plates. I told her she would come to grief. Is that what—"

"I am talking about plates for counterfeit money, Papa."

"Counterfeit money? I know nothing about that." His baffled expression told her he spoke the truth. "But I wager a fellow called Dooley had a finger in it. He used to be a friend of Prissie's when she first came to London. He has been hounding the poor girl, threatening to run to Bow Street over the Dürer business, which is why she destroyed those plates."

"Dooley is mixed up in it. I believe he killed her."

Sir John was silent a moment. When he spoke, it was not about the business at hand. "Where did you hear about Dooley? I don't want you to have anything to do with the scoundrel, Lydia. Good God! How did you get mixed up in any of this? How did you learn Prissie and I were . . . associated?"

"She went to Kesterly to see you. She asked directions to Trevelyn Hall the last time she left the inn. Did you meet her there? I know you were not so ill as you let on, Papa."

"I did not meet her. I didn't know for sure she had gone until yesterday. I knew she had been worried about Dooley for some time now. He wanted her to do some forging job for him. She refused, and was afraid what he might do in revenge. She wrote me, here at Grosvenor Square, that she wanted to get out of town. I went to call on her. She was so upset—actually afraid for her life!—that I went home to the Hall at once to look about for a little cottage where she would be safe. Meanwhile she had to call on a friend in the country." Lydia mentally said, Richie!

Sir John continued. "She was to go to the inn in Kesterly after her country visit. The estate agent who was handling the matter for me was to notify her there. She registered under a different name, of course. We had arranged that I would stay at the Hall until the matter was settled. I took to my bed, claiming an attack of gout. Truth to tell, I needed

137

the rest. I have been working pretty hard, and with the strain of wondering if I would get the appointment to the Cabinet, I was about ready to collapse. I feared that Dooley might make trouble for me as well if I returned to London. And just when I could least afford a scandal. I wouldn't put it a pace past the weasel. All things considered, it seemed best to rusticate for a spell."

"Prissie did make the plates. She needed the money. You must not have been very generous, Papa," she said with an angry look.

"I kept her in decent style. I am not a nabob after all, and naturally my own family must come first. She knew that when we . . . became friends."

"When you took her under your protection, you mean. You did not protect her very well, did you?" Sir John gave a wince of pain or guilt. "How long ago did you and she become friends?"

"Ten years ago, when your mama told me definitely she had no interest in coming to London, even for the Season. She used to accompany me for a few months a year at least. We had a great, thundering row about it. I could not budge her an inch, and I didn't feel I could give up my work in politics. I did not want to become a country squire. Politics was my—half my life. Prissie and I came to terms at that time, and I have never welshed on our bargain."

"What about Richie?" she asked, and observed her father closely. The name came as no surprise to him. He knew about Prissie's son.

"So you know about Richie. What about him?" he asked brusquely.

"Do you support him as well?"

"He is no concern of mine. What business have

138

you to question me in this way? Have I not been a good father to you? What have you ever lacked that money could buy, or love for that matter?"

"I lacked a father for ten months of the year!" she flashed back. "You never even came home for my birthday—or Mama's. You might have spared us a day at least."

"I came as often as my work allowed, Lydia. It was not Prissie who kept me away. Perhaps I was overly ambitious in my career. I thought you understood, if your mama did not."

When he shook his head sadly at her, she rushed into his arms and hugged him. "I'm sorry, Papa. I just thought—"

"That I didn't love you?" he asked, with a rueful, sad smile. "I wanted you—you all—to be proud of me."

"We are! I know it was not all your fault. I should have—and Mama—"

"Don't blame yourself. And don't blame Miriam. She was a fish out of water in London. She hated it. People do what they must and can do. That's the sum and total of it. It was an unfortunate marriage. But that is the way when the heart rules. Think twice before you marry, Lydia, and make sure it is not mere infatuation. That doesn't last a year. And what is this I hear of you and Beaumont, eh? Does he know of my . . . troubles?"

"Yes, he's been helping me."

"Pity. I hope it don't put him off offering."

"Beau and I are just friends, Papa. Pray don't say anything to him to suggest we expect an offer."

Her father gave her a long, penetrating look. "So it is young Beaumont who has been ferreting around in my past, is it? Finding out about my

139

association with Prissie. I am relieved to hear it, though I am sorry he told you. For a moment there, I feared you had been talking to the muslin company. I know I can depend on Beaumont's discretion. He is a man of the world."

Lydia left her father under the comfortable illusion that Beau had been doing all the hobnobbing with the demimonde. She felt her father had taken enough blows for one day. Before leaving, she said, "Prissie didn't give you a parcel to look after for her?"

"You are thinking of the counterfeit plates? No, I didn't even know she had made them. Poor girl. If she needed more money, she should have told me. I could have found some funds. But she was never a grasping sort of girl. Just a sweet country lass who went astray. She reminded me a little of your mama when she was young—in her looks, I mean. Only in her looks. Poor Prissie, I shall miss her. I sent her mother a check to tend to the burial expenses."

They were interrupted by a tap at the door. Nessie poked her head in. "Lord Castlereagh to see you, John. He's waiting in the saloon."

"I'll be right there. We'll talk later, Lydia." He left.

"Beaumont is here as well," Nessie said, twinkling a smile at Lydia. "Has he come to speak to your papa?"

"No! Don't get your hopes up, Nessie."

Nessie just continued smiling. All was well with her world. Castlereagh had invited her and John to an intimate dinner party on the weekend. Before John's promotion, they had been invited only to the Foreign Secretary's large parties. They were now part of the inner circle that ruled the country.

140

When they went into the saloon, Beaumont was just offering Sir John his congratulations.

Castlereagh, who had an eye for young ladies, said a few words to Lydia; then Sir John led him down the hall to his study, and Nessie returned to her correspondence.

"Did you come for any special reason, Beau?" Lydia asked when they were alone. She feared he would have some unpleasant news regarding Dooley.

"You certainly know how to make a fellow feel welcome! And after you asked me particularly last night if I would not be calling this morning."

"Did I? I don't remember." Last night seemed a year ago. But she was glad he was here. She felt the need of someone to share her troubles, and Beau had been a friend for as long as she could remember. "Since you're here, we might as well go out."

"I am underwhelmed by your enthusiasm. And I am wearing a new jacket, too."

"It's very nice," she said, just glancing at it. Beau was always so well dressed that she hadn't noticed it was new.

"No one will ever accuse you of flattery, Lydia. Well, as your mind is on business, did you speak with Sir John?"

"We'll talk outside."

She got her bonnet, and they escaped into the sunshine.

"You might have warned me your papa is here," Beaumont said, as he helped her into his carriage. "I believe he expected me to crop out into an offer, coming at such an early hour of the day."

"Never mind that. We have more important things to discuss. Prissie did not give Papa the plates." She repeated to him what she had learned

141

from Sir John. "We must get busy and find them before Dooley does. He is so determined to get them, I'm sure we can think of some way to catch him if we have the plates for a lure."

"When I first suggested that clever idea last night, you had no interest in it."

"Well, I have now. He isn't going to get off scotfree with killing Prissie. And we have to do something about Richie as well, Beau."

"He is your papa's son, then?"

"I was about to ask when Papa decided to mount his high horse and deliver me a scold. As he has been Prissie's patron for a decade, however, it looks as if I have a half brother. And by the by, Papa thinks you are the one who has been doing all the investigating."

"Why, thank you for that. I'm sure it has raised his opinion of me no end, particularly that I went running to pour the tale into his daughter's shelllike ear. Such a finely tuned sense of discretion will do my reputation no end of good."

"Don't be so selfish," she scolded. "What should we do about Richie? Papa didn't show an iota of surprise or confusion when I mentioned him. Richie must be his by-blow. An illegitimate son, imagine!"

"These things happen, even in the best-regulated families. Even the royal family. *En effet,* especially in the royal family. Do you have a destination in mind, or are we just driving?"

"St. John's Wood. That is where Richie is being raised, with some people called the Nevils. I'll know to look at him whether he is my brother. And if he is, I shall adopt him."

Beaumont just stared. "Will you also adopt a papa

142

to go with him? Children are usually adopted by a set of parents, not a spinster."

"In that case, I shall make Papa adopt him."

"How will you do that?"

"I have learned a few tricks from my new friends. I shall threaten Papa with revealing his shameful behavior to Mama. Don't laugh at me, Beaumont. I am serious!"

"A reformer shouldn't be so pretty," he said. "And so headstrong. Would it not be advisable to discuss this adoption with Sir John before visiting this soi-disant half brother, who may be no kin to you whatsoever? There is your mother to consider in the matter as well."

"Yes, she must be kept in the dark. Perhaps we can claim he is one of Nessie's orphans. Would you like to talk to Papa for me, Beau?" she asked. "He will only scold at me and tell me it is none of my concern. He thinks you're a man of the world. He'll speak more freely to you."

"No, I would not like to." She gave a sulky, accusing look, like a child who has been denied a sugarplum. Her lower lip protruded; then she bit it with her little white teeth. "But I might do it, if you ask me very nicely."

He watched in fascination as her sulky expression transformed into a smile. She cocked her head at a flirtatious angle, batted her long eyelashes, and turned up her lips softly. "Please. Pretty please," she said in a wheedling way that made him smile in spite of knowing he was being managed. Was it only a few days ago he had thought she didn't know how to deal with men?

He gazed at her a long moment. He could almost think she was literally growing up before his very eyes. A moment ago she had seemed a child. But she had a fully mature sense of duty. And now, with that teasing smile lifting her lips and her eyes laughing at him (she knew he would do it for her) she was all woman, and a very tantalizing woman.

"Do you know, Lydia Trevelyn, you are becoming amazingly coquettish for a spinster. Very well, I'll do it . . . for you. But I may demand some payment."

"You can count on me to help you out of any difficulty when your future wife discovers your mistress," she said.

"Thank you, Miss Trevelyn, for that reading of my character." He was ready to mount his high horse, until he saw the laughter in her eyes. "And I shall reciprocate by providing you an alibi when you begin to deceive your husband."

"You forget, I am going to be a spinster," she said, and laughed.

Chapter Fourteen

They went for a drive through Hyde Park to enjoy the beauty of spring, but with so much on her mind, Lydia could not appreciate the blue sky and golden sunshine, the whispering trees and the gleaming water of the Serpentine.

"Let us go back to Grosvenor Square for that talk with Papa," she suggested.

"Business before pleasure, eh? Very well."

When they reached Grosvenor Square, Nessie told them Sir John had left for Whitehall with Castlereagh and did not expect to be back before dinner. She was surrounded by half a dozen ladies, come to congratulate the new rising star of political hostesses. The Countess deLieven, Princess Esterhazy, Lady Jersey—the very cream of society were there welcoming her to their charmed circle.

The ladies raised their eyebrows in speculation when Beaumont and Lydia came in together. A delightful new on dit would soon be making the rounds. Lord Beaumont and Sir John's daughter were about to make a match! He was running tame at Grosvenor Square. Beaumont was subjected to some good-natured bantering by the outspoken Countess deLieven.

"No grass growing under your feet, Beaumont.

You do your courting early in the day. Beating the crowd to Miss Trevelyn's door, sly dog!"

"Had I known you were up so early, ma'am, I would have invited you to join us," Beaumont replied flirtatiously. "Miss Trevelyn would have had formidable competition."

"A flirt!" She laughed in delight. "You don't want to let this sly rogue loose in female company until you have the ring on your finger, Miss Trevelyn." She glanced to see if Lydia wore an engagement ring.

"You are perfectly welcome to him, milady," Lydia said, joining in the game. "I have no use for flirts."

"There, you see, Beaumont!" Lady deLieven said. "Fair warning. She is not interested in flirting. Run for your life if you are not interested in marriage."

"Only if Miss Trevelyn will run with me," he said, and taking Lydia's hand, he escaped from the room.

"Why did you say that?" Lydia scolded, when they were away from prying ears. "You only encourage her to start spreading gossip."

"My sweet ninnyhammer, this particular piece of gossip is a fait accompli. You had best begin planning either a wedding or a jilting. Bearing in mind that I am the innocent party, you must be at pains not to sully my reputation in the process."

"You have only to go about looking morose after I return to the Hall, and the whole will be dumped in my dish." She drew a deep sigh. "I can't think of anything useful to do at the moment. You might as well go, Beau."

"Giving me my congé so soon? What will you do for the rest of the day?"

"I shall go back to Maddox Street and see if Sally has anything new to say. We didn't ask her specifically about a small, heavyish parcel. Prissie might have left it with her for safekeeping."

"You can't go there alone!" he exclaimed.

"Now don't you start acting like Papa. I thought you were different."

"Not that different!" He lowered his brows at her. He knew she resented Sir John's authority, and was unhappy to be put in the same boat with him, but still he could not let a young lady wander alone into such questionable purlieus as Maddox Street. "I don't plan to be left out of the investigation," he prevaricated. "Let us go together. And Lydia—"

"Yes?"

"Ask Blake to tell your aunt you aren't sure when you'll be back. We don't know what we might find there. That will leave us free to follow where our noses take us."

"Nessie is so caught up in Papa's promotion, she wouldn't notice if I disappeared into the ether." But still it was nice to have the freedom of movement a male escort allowed. If she had gone alone, Nessie would be worried. Just another example of how unfair society was.

She got her bonnet and left the message with Blake, and they returned to Beaumont's waiting carriage for the drive to Maddox Street. Halfway there, Lydia realized Beaumont was staring at her in a disapproving way.

"What's the matter? Why are you looking at me like that?"

"Your toilette. It's all wrong."

Lydia, who had formerly disdained any interest in fancy toilette, felt a sting of anger. She had noticed how well dressed the ladies calling on Nessie were.

She had felt like a country bumpkin beside them. "I don't claim to be a lady of fashion," she said.

"I am well aware of it, but that was not my meaning. You look like a lady, even if not a lady of fashion. A lightskirt would not be caught dead in that bonnet. When you visited Sally yesterday, your head was bare. You were wearing that old gown of Prissie's."

"I'll change when we get there."

"Why bother? A garish bonnet will serve the purpose. We'll pick one up at one of the inferior milliners on the fringe of New Bond Street."

"I see you are familiar with where the lightskirts buy their bonnets." She sniffed.

"Any bonnet I purchased for a woman would be from Mademoiselle Fancot's—tip of the ton. But that is not where Prissie and her friends buy theirs. I happen to have heard of another establishment."

She gave him a rebukeful look but did not rise to the bait. "I hope you treat your women better than Papa did. He should have taken better care of Prissie when he knew Dooley was harassing her. Expensive bonnets are all well and good, but they don't last. And furthermore, I do not need a new bonnet. A bunch of flowers attached to this one will serve the purpose as well."

"I shall agree with you, before you inform me 'a penny saved is a penny earned.' " He drew the check string and told the driver to deliver them to New Bond Street. They dismounted and strolled along, looking for a shop that sold novelties. Lydia was struck again by how elegant the ladies looked—and how friendly they were to Beaumont. It seemed everyone they met spoke to him. Some tried to stop for a chat.

148

When they found the shop they wanted, they went in and scanned the artificial flowers.

"This is rather nice," Lydia said, picking up a discreet bunch of lilacs.

"For a maiden aunt. Try this." He handed her a large cluster of scarlet poppies.

"I can't wear that! I'll look like a— Oh, very well. I'll need a box of pins as well."

When Beaumont drew out his purse, she gave him a damping look and handed the clerk the money herself.

"All set for Maddox Street?" Beaumont said, when they left the shop.

"No, I want to buy a present for Richie. I wonder what a little boy would like."

"Toy soldiers, a ball, a toy sailing boat, if he has access to water," he suggested, thinking back to his own youth.

"Prissie bought him a sailor suit. I'll buy him a toy boat. There's bound to be a pond or creek nearby."

They strolled along, looking for a children's toy store. The store had only two models of sailing vessels: one small, cheap boat and a beautiful scale model replica of the *Princess Margaret*, two feet long, fully rigged and painted, that cost three pounds.

"I'll take this one," she said, smiling softly. "Poor Richie deserves a few treats at this sad time. I wonder if he knows yet. . . ."

When Beaumont, watching her, saw the tears well in her eyes, he felt a strong urge to take her in his arms and comfort her. Where had he got the idea Lydia Trevelyn was made of granite? Her heart was as soft as cotton wool. And all this for a boy she had never met, or heard of, until yesterday. How much more deeply hurt she must have felt when she considered her father's betrayal.

The ship proved so difficult to wrap that Beaumont carried it unwrapped to the carriage, encountering many curious stares and a few jibes from acquaintances as he went. The ship was placed carefully on the banquette, with Beaumont sitting beside it, holding it in place while Lydia tended to her bonnet. Beaumont's lips moved in silent amusement as she bent over the task, frowning as intently as if she were solving a difficult problem in algebra.

When she had the poppies pinned in place, she put the bonnet on and said, "How does it look?"

"You look wretched, like a little girl who was let loose in a milliner's shop."

"I didn't say how do I look. I know I look a quiz beside the other ladies. Especially Lady Jersey. What I want to know is how the bonnet looks."

"Suitably awful."

"Good, then we can go to Maddox Street now."

"Don't put your head to the window," he said. "You'll destroy my reputation if you're seen in my rig wearing that flower garden."

"Vain creature! You're the one who wanted poppies," she scolded, and leaned closer to the window to annoy him, unaware that he was biting back a grin.

They continued on to Maddox Street, where Beaumont told the coachman to keep the carriage waiting while they went into Prissie's flat.

"You wait here in her parlor," she said. "I'll call on Sally. She'll speak more freely if we're alone."

Before he sat down, there was a tap at the door and Sally let herself in.

"Nancy!" she cried. "I've been that worried about you! I've called half a dozen times and got no answer. I just heard the door open and came right over. Where were you last night? I saw you leave the Pantheon with Dooley. I hope you're not with him." Then she saw Beaumont, who had taken up a seat on the sofa. "Oh, sorry, Nance. I didn't know you had company."

Beaumont rose and bowed. Lydia was pleased that he showed this mark of respect for Sally. Sally worked a fan she was carrying and simpered over the top of it. "I am the culprit who spirited Nancy away," he said.

"Have you set her up?"

"Er—yes."

Sally found a chair and Beaumont sat down beside Lydia. He took her hand, to lend an aura of romance to affairs. Sally began batting her fan diligently.

"In better digs than this, I warrant," she said. "Haven't you landed in the honeypot, Nancy! Mind you, I can't complain. My Mr. Warner gave me this fan last night. It's real ivory! Ever so pretty, isn't it?" She handed it to Lydia, who praised it until Sally was satisfied, then set it aside. "Have you heard from Prissie?"

"Not yet. I plan to go to St. John's Wood this afternoon. I'll let you know what I find there. Sally, did Prissie happen to leave a parcel with you before she left? It would be a smallish, heavy parcel."

"No, she didn't." She narrowed her eyes in suspicion. "Why, what's in it?"

"A present for Richie. I thought I would take it to him this afternoon."

151

"If it was for Richie, you can be sure she took it with her. Sure it wasn't something else?"

"Why do you say that?"

"Because Dooley was around early this morning asking the same question. He asked a lot of questions about you as well, Nance. Had the notion Prissie's sister had blond hair." She frowned at Lydia's raven curls but was soon distracted by the bonnet.

"My hair was lighter when I was young," Lydia said.

Sally picked up her fan and resumed her fanning. "Dooley searched my flat last night while I was out. Or someone did. Tell the truth now, Nancy. What was he looking for? Was Prissie up to her old tricks?"

"I'm afraid she was," Lydia said, and listened to hear if Sally knew about the counterfeiting.

"Gorblimey, I hope the law hasn't caught her with the evidence on her or she'll swing for sure. It's a pity she ever learned how to do it, work with them copper plates. She made me swear not to tell a soul. I wasn't sure if you knew or not."

"How did she learn?" Lydia asked.

Sally's eyebrows drew together in a quick, suspicious frown. She studied Lydia's dark curls. "It's what she was doing for that artist fellow before she left home, isn't it? Funny her own sister wouldn't know that."

"She never done banknotes," Lydia said, to cover her gaffe.

Sally seemed satisfied with this. "That's true. She never did. I wager Dooley took her to someone to learn the fine points of that. The fellow who was doing it for him and Wilkie got put into Newgate for

passing bad bills. He'll be doing the hangman's jig."
This awful fate was mentioned casually in passing.
It was obviously a feature of life in Sally's set. "Why
don't you two and me and my gent get together
tonight?"

"I'm not sure what Beau has in mind," Lydia said,
looking at Beaumont. She wanted to say something
to convince Sally she was who she claimed to be.
With a memory of the red feathers on Prissie's
bonnet, she added, "Now that you've bought me this
nice bonnet, I want to show it off. Wouldn't Prissie
love it. Red, her favorite color."

"Nancy and I had planned an evening alone,
Sally," he said, putting a possessive arm around
Lydia's shoulder and drawing her to his side. Lydia
stiffened at this familiarity, until she realized it was
part of the act; then she tried to relax. But it felt
strange, being pressed close against Beau's hard,
masculine body, with his fingers tugging playfully
at her curls. Strange and exciting.

Sally gave him a knowing grin. "I see you two
want to be alone. Three's company, as they say. If I
hear anything about the plates, I'll let you know."
She rose and began to tidy her skirt. "Where's your
new flat, Nance?"

Lydia just stared. She was familiar with only the
polite part of London.

"We haven't quite decided," Beaumont said.
"We're looking at a place on Harrowby Street this
afternoon, but you can send word to my place, Manchester Square. Nancy won't be home much. She
plans to spend her day shopping. I'll see she gets the
message."

"Lucky Nancy! Shopping all day."

"I need a great many things. I brought very little

153

with me," Lydia said. She began to rise to accompany Sally to the door.

"Don't bother. I'll let myself out," Sally said, and left.

"You can let me go now," Lydia said to Beaumont as soon as they were alone.

"Not yet," he said, his arm tightening around her. She looked at him in surprise, which grew to alarm as she read the mischievous gleam in his eyes.

"Let me go, Beau! What are you doing?"

"Just what any gent would do when he's alone with his chère amie," he said, and wrapping his arms around her tightly, he kissed her full on the lips. Not a gentle buss, but a firm kiss that frightened her with its ardor.

Lydia's first reaction was shock, which quickly changed to anger at this show of lechery. She pushed at his shoulders, but he only tightened his arms around her until she was held helpless against the assault of his lips. A strangely persuasive assault that had the curious effect of turning her insides to molten honey, all hot and sweet. She felt her heart pound against his chest; it reverberated in her ears and throat like a vast, throbbing engine.

Overcome by this unexpected turn of events, Lydia didn't hear the door opening, and Sally came pattering back into the parlor.

"Oh, sorry!" Sally said, laughing.

Beaumont released Lydia then. She looked at him in confusion, with a dazed expression on her face.

"Forgot my fan," Sally said, picking it up from the table. "Carry on, folks. Don't mind me. You ain't doing nothing I haven't done." She ran out, laughing.

Lydia was about to chastise Beaumont, but something in his expression stopped her. He was waiting for her to make a fool of herself. He had that self-congratulatory look in his eyes. He had known Sally would be coming back. That's why he had kissed her, to convince Sally they were lovers.

"Her fan," he said. "I noticed she left it behind. No point in fanning her suspicion that you're not Nancy Shepherd. No pun intended."

"That—that's quite all right, Beau," she said in a choked voice. She cleared her throat and added primly, "No doubt you know best how gentlemen behave in such circumstances, but I think a peck on the cheek would have done as well."

A slow smile spread across his lips; it rose to soften his eyes. "But it wouldn't have been as much fun, would it?" he said in a softly insinuating voice that sent ripples of excitement trembling up her spine.

Lydia took a deep breath to steady her own voice and said, "Fun? I can't imagine what you're talking about. Well, we know Sally doesn't have the plates. Shall we go?"

"Spoilsport," he chided gently, and rose, laughing.

Chapter Fifteen

"We might as well go to St. John's Wood," Lydia said, when they were back in the carriage. "I shan't say anything about adopting Richie. I just want to see him—give him the boat." She removed her bonnet and began unpinning the poppies. "Poor tyke. I wish—Beau, would you mind driving to Whitehall first? If Papa is free, we could have a word with him before we go, and find out what his intentions are regarding Richie. You don't have to do it. I'll talk to him."

"That might be best," he agreed, and directed his driver to take them to Whitehall. "I'll ask Sir John to come out to the carriage. This conversation had best take place where no one can overhear it."

Lydia waited in the carriage while Beaumont went inside. While she sat alone, she planned what to say to her father. She was surprised to see her neighbor Horace Findley go into the building. No doubt he was in London on business and had stopped by to congratulate Sir John. She felt a pang for poor Horace, who had recently suffered the loss of his wife. And, unlike her father, he had no son to carry on the name and estate. That was one definite disadvantage to not marrying, never to have a child of one's own. Horace had seemed to age ten years when his wife died, but he was recovering now. There was a livelier spring in his step.

As the minutes dragged on, she drew out her comb and mirror and began to fix her hair. The bonnet looked dowdy without its poppies. She pinned one discreet flower on the brim. Just the one gave the bonnet an air of jaunty distinction. She put the bonnet back on, using her mirror to arrange it at a saucy angle that was more attractive. She thought Beau would approve. Perhaps she should buy a new bonnet before returning to Trevelyn Hall. Why had she thought she must dress so plainly because she planned to be a spinster? It was that sort of asceticism that gave spinsters their dreary reputation. She would buy two bonnets, and some new muslin as well. That was a pretty shade Princess Esterhazy had been wearing—yellow, but a soft creamy yellow, with green ribbons.

Quite half an hour had passed before Beau came out, and he was alone.

"It's impossible to get a moment with Sir John," he said. "He is at an important meeting with Liverpool and company. I hadn't the courage to barge into the Prime Minister's office."

"Then we shall go on to St. John's Wood without seeing him." She waited for his reaction to the bonnet.

He said, "Horace Findley was there trying for a word with him as well. I wonder what brings him to London."

"Poor man." She touched her fingers to the brim of her bonnet, as if adjusting it. "I shall call on him when I return. He must be lonesome without his wife."

Beaumont noticed Lydia was looking at him

expectantly, and wondered what caused it. "Is there anything else we must do before we leave? Do you want to have a word with your aunt?"

"No, nothing," she said, and tossed her head aside in annoyance. He hadn't even noticed the poppy!

"You might as well tell me, Lydia. It is a longish trip. No need to suffer it in silence."

"It's nothing. Nothing at all. If I am quiet, it is just that I am thinking of Richie. Do be careful of the boat, Beau! You nearly knocked that sail off."

She looked out the window as they began the drive out of London. Beau removed his curled beaver and leaned against the velvet squabs of the banquette. "Might as well be comfortable," he said. "Why don't you take your bonnet off as well? It looks nice, the way you've put that one flower on. Rather chic. Less is more, in ornamentation."

She looked at him then, with a small smile of satisfaction curving her lips. That's what she was after, the minx! She wanted a compliment on the bonnet. It did look rather saucy, in a sweet way.

"This?" she said, removing the hat and looking at it nonchalantly. "I thought it needed a touch of color." She put it aside and began to talk in a more natural way about Richie, and what she would like to do for him.

"Since I don't plan to have any children of my own, I shall take an interest in his welfare."

"You have quite determined not to have children of your own, then?" he said, and studied her with keen interest, until she felt heat bloom on her cheeks. Having proclaimed her firm decision not to marry, she now found it difficult to change her tune, lest Beau think she was dangling after him.

158

"Since I don't intend to marry, it is not likely I shall have children."

"I want half a dozen," he said. "Three boys and three girls. It was lonesome, being an only child."

"I might as well have been an only child. Only one brother, and he was always with a tutor or at school or doing boy things."

"Pity you hadn't taken up fishing earlier."

"Somehow I don't think that would have pleased Tom. And I know Mama hates it. She feels my only job is to find a husband."

"And you, being a rebel, have dug in your heels and decided against marriage—and children? Cut off your nose to spite your face, in fact."

"It wasn't quite that simple. I just don't want the sort of marriage Mama has. I might marry one day, if I ever happen to meet the right man." She was careful not to look within a right angle of Beaumont as she delivered this speech, and thus did not see that he was studying her with the keenest interest.

"Somehow, I don't think your marriage would be like Lady Trevelyn's," he said, trying not to laugh.

"I hope not. If I did marry, I would want at least two boys and two girls."

"That will make quite a crowd in the neighborhood. Six of mine and four of yours."

She smiled into the distance. "I can just see them, all playing by the river."

"Still trying to catch Finny," he said, nodding. "I thought I had hooked him, that day we found Prissie's body."

"I shan't tell my children about finding Prissie there. It will only put them off fishing."

He noticed that she spoke about her future children in a way that was unusual for a young lady who had been a determined spinster the day before. "They'll love it! Children adore horror stories."

"Boys do, you mean."

He took his curled beaver and set it on her head. "Are you admitting there is a difference between the sexes now, Lydia?" he asked, studying her.

"Of course there is. Girls are much nicer," she riposted, and put her bonnet on him. "Very fetching, Beau. You will start a new style if anyone sees you."

He removed the bonnet. "A handsome gent looks good in anything."

The trip passed quickly in the easy banter of old friends. As they drew closer to St. John's Wood, Lydia became quiet.

"I wonder what sort of home he was raised in," she said. "I hope it is respectable. Poor Prissie hadn't much money."

"I'll enquire at the next farm for the Nevils' address."

They drove on for a quarter of a mile. On the right, Lydia saw a pretty half-timbered and stucco cottage with pink roses growing over the facade. A young man was just coming from the stable, mounted on a gray cob. She took him for the owner, and hailed him. At closer range, she saw he was quite young, not more than thirteen or fourteen, but with broad shoulders and wearing a blue jacket and a curled beaver. His being on horseback had fooled her as to his size and age.

"I am looking for the Nevils," she said. "Do they live near here?"

"This is the Nevils' place," he said, lifting his hat and bowing politely.

"Oh!" She smiled her pleasure to discover Richie lived in such good circumstances. The cottage was small, but more than respectable. Cows grazed in the pasture beyond it. The barns and outbuildings were in good repair, and this young man was well spoken.

"Is there a young lad called Richie living here?"

"I'm Richard," he replied, his curiosity rising.

"You!" she cried, astonished to see her little half brother was bigger than she was.

"Did you wish to see me, or the Nevils?" he asked.

"You! It is you I wished to see." She hardly knew how to continue after this shock. The boy was obviously not her papa's child. Papa had known Prissie for only ten years. But the lad still must be told of Prissie's death. And she would still do something to help him. "I am a friend of Prissie Shepherd."

His eyes moved in an assessing manner over her, the carriage, and Beaumont. "You don't look like her other friends," he said. "Are you an actress, too?"

Beaumont decided it was time to get out of the carriage for easier conversing and Lydia followed him. Richie dismounted and the three of them stood together.

"No, not exactly an actress," Lydia said uncertainly. "I have something to tell you about Prissie, Richard."

"Aunt Prissie told me she would be leaving London and couldn't visit me for a while," he said. "I hope she is not ill?"

Beaumont and Lydia exchanged a questioning look. "Your aunt Prissie?" Beaumont asked.

"Yes. I am an orphan. Did you not know? When Papa died, I was placed with the Nevils. Aunt Prissie visits every week, and my uncle comes as often as he can. They are not husband and wife. Prissie is my aunt on my mama's side; my uncle is

161

from my papa's side. Now that his wife has died, he wants me to go and live with him. Lonesome, I daresay. He has no children. What were you saying about Prissie?"

They began walking toward the cottage, with Richard leading his mount.

"I'm afraid she met with an accident, Richard," Beaumont said. "She was drowned."

"How horrible!" Richard cried. He was obviously shocked and sorry, yet not so sorry as if he'd known she was his mother. "When did it happen? Is there anything I can do? I wonder if Uncle Horace knows."

"I'm not sure," Beaumont said. He looked at Lydia, who was looking at him with a question growing in her eyes. "What is your uncle's last name?" Beaumont asked, although he already had an inkling.

Richard looked at them, surprised. "Why, Horace Findley. Did Prissie not tell you? I am Richard Findley."

Lydia gasped. Horace Findley! That model husband, the grieving widower.

To cover her shock, Beaumont said, "Findley, of course. That was the name," and nodded, as if it had merely slipped his mind. "So, you will be joining your uncle Horace. I daresay you are looking forward to that."

"The Nevils have been very kind. I would not say a word against them, but family is more—intimate," he said, choosing the word with care. "And, of course, as I am to inherit my uncle's estate, it is only fitting that I should learn how to run it, now that I am growing up. But I am most distressed to hear about Aunt Prissie. How did it happen? A boating accident?"

Lydia felt it was up to Horace Findley to decide

what his son should be told. "I'm not sure," she said. "A friend of Prissie's told me of her death. I was very sorry to hear of it."

As the shock of Richard's true father ebbed, Lydia remembered the other reason she had come. "The last time your aunt was here, did she bring a parcel with her? She didn't leave anything with you?"

"She did bring a little box, but she didn't leave it with me."

She had to quell her excitement, for she did not want to incite Richard to suspicion. "Do you know what she did with it?"

He pointed behind the house, into the distance on his left. "There's a pond back there. She threw it into the pond. She didn't know I saw her. She did it before she came to the house. I happened to be at my bedroom window. I asked her about it. It was just some old love letters she wanted to be rid of. She weighted them down with stones and threw them in the pond. It's not very deep, but I didn't pull them out. I didn't think I should look at them—and besides, they'd be all waterlogged," he added less nobly. "She couldn't throw them very far, being only a woman."

Lydia just shook her head. How early this easy assumption of masculine superiority set in.

"Well, as long as the letters are safely disposed of," Beaumont said, with a meaningful glance at Lydia.

"Who were they from?" Richard asked.

Lydia said in confusion, "I—I really couldn't say."

"I know Aunt Prissie had a beau. Well, a patron, to be frank. She was an actress, you know. A little unconventional, but a jolly good sort. The letters must have been—interesting, for he sent some

163

fellow after them. He broke into the house one night. I'm sure that is what he was after. This isn't the sort of house the ken smashers break into. As if Prissie would publish them or sell them. P'raps she just told him that for a lark. She was a great one for jokes."

Lydia thought of her mama, who never joked or laughed. Prissie must have been a welcome change for her papa. She felt they had learned what they came to learn and was eager to be alone with Beaumont to discuss recovering the plates. She assumed it was the plates Prissie had cast into the pond, not letters.

Richard invited them in for tea. "Mrs. Nevil would like to meet you," he said.

"We are in a bit of a hurry, but pray do give her my regards," Lydia said.

Richard accompanied them back to the carriage and looked with interest at the crest on its panel. "I don't believe I caught your name, ma'am."

"We're the Beaumonts," Beaumont said, and shook Richard's hand.

Richard studied the crest a moment; then he looked inside the carriage. "I say! What a handsome ship model! Is it yours, milord? I noticed the crest on your door panel," he added, with a knowing smile. "I thought the letters must be from you, but any gentleman with such a lovely young wife would not be writing to another woman." This was accompanied by a bow in Lydia's direction.

"Nor would I be fool enough to bring my wife on an errand to recover them," Beaumont replied. "Milady has quite a temper, and is jealous as a green cow."

"And you, milord, have a marvelous imagination.

The ship is for you, Richard," Lydia said, feeling foolish as she handed it to him. It must have been several years ago that Prissie bought that sailor suit for her son. "A—bequest from your aunt Prissie."

"Oh, I say! What a handsome gift!" he exclaimed, smiling and examining it. "It is just like Aunt Prissie. She always knew exactly what I wanted. I didn't even know she owned such a thing. I shall treasure it."

"I'm glad you like it. And now we had best leave, Beau."

Richard waved them off, standing by his gray cob, holding the model of the *Princess Margaret* under one arm.

"There's a bit of a shocker!" Beaumont said, as the carriage lurched into motion.

"At least he liked the boat," she said, and dissolved into a fit of nervous giggles.

Chapter Sixteen

"Relieved Richard isn't your brother?" Beaumont asked, as they drove back to London.

"Relieved, disappointed, too," she said with a wistful smile. "He seems a nice boy. Fancy old Horace Findley!"

"What has happened to your self-righteous indignation? This siring of illegitimate sons was a greater crime when Sir John was the culprit."

"What is Horace Findley to me?" she replied with a shrug. "I can't change the world, but I expect better from my own father."

"You've abrogated the parents' role to yourself. It is usually the father who expects better from his children. But then I daresay you never caused Sir John a single sleepless night—until now, I mean."

"It was Mama who lost sleep over me, due to my lack of interest in marriage. It sounded so excessively boring, all duty and no fun."

"Did she never tell you some of those duties can be amusing?" he asked, with a smile she could not quite trust. His lips were unsteady, but when she looked into his eyes, she saw something more serious. When she failed to reply, he said, "We'll soon have Richard for a neighbor. He'll be surprised Lord and Lady Beaumont occupy separate houses."

"We'll have to have a word with him, convince him he misunderstood."

"Either that, or get married," Beau replied reasonably.

Lydia gave him a long, silent look. Was he joking? Did he feel he had compromised her by being seen with her around London? Did he just feel it was time to settle down, now that he had begun his political life? A father-in-law in the Cabinet would be a help to his career, but somehow she couldn't think Beau was that devious. Was it possible he actually loved her? She could tell nothing from his impassive face.

He waited to hear how she reacted to this notion, but when she spoke, she said, "We are not the only ones who will have some explaining to do. I wonder how Findley will explain his son to the neighborhood."

Beaumont felt a sting of disappointment. Most ladies would have made that the start of an excellent flirtation. "Nephew," he said. "That is the story he told Richard."

"Horace doesn't have a brother."

"He has a sister, has he not?"

"Yes, a spinster who lives in Tunbridge Wells. His wife, Alice, had some siblings, and he has various cousins. Beau!" She sat upright and grabbed his arm. "That is what Horace was doing at the House this morning, wanting to see Papa. He was warning him that he meant to adopt Richard, and that he must not blow the gaff. I wonder how it all happened, Horace jilting Prissie, and Papa taking her on."

"The two gentlemen are friends. It is not unusual for a gent to arrange a new patron when he gives his mistress her congé. Don't scowl at me! I am merely explaining how it might have happened. I daresay your papa met her through Horace in any case."

"Yes, I don't see how else he would have met a woman like that. Not that I mean to denigrate her, but they would not travel in the same circles."

They drove on a while in silence while each considered how this new development affected the case.

"About the plates—" Beaumont said.

Lydia understood him at once. "After dark," she replied. "We shall go back after dark and fish them out of the pond."

"That leaves Dooley off scot-free." He sat, frowning a moment. "Unless . . ." They exchanged a speaking glance.

Lydia said, "Unless we can convince him to steal them from us, and have Bow Street catch him with the plates in his possession. All we have to do is let him know we have them. He'll do the rest."

"We must do it in such a way that he doesn't smell a trap."

"He already knows I am not Nancy. He was quizzing Sally about me. It seems Nancy is a blonde. Prissie mentioned it to him. He knows I have some interest in all this. I think he would believe it if I let it be known I have the plates."

"Too dangerous," he said at once.

"We must arrange it in some safe manner. I'll let him know I'm Sir John's daughter, that Prissie left a parcel with him for safekeeping, not telling him what was in it, of course. I opened the parcel and realized the possibilities of the plates. I am interested in selling them to the highest bidder. He already suspects I'm no better than I should be, after my appearance at the Pantheon. I could say I am in the suds and need the money desperately to—to—what?"

"Buy back some indiscreet love letters?" he suggested.

"Or pay my gambling debts."

"It's still dangerous. And how could we let him know all this?"

She thought a moment, then said, "Sally could act as our go-between. She sees him from time to time. Let us go and have a chat with Sally."

"You're playing with fire, Miss Trevelyn," Sally said, when they opened their budget to her, explaining what they had been doing, and outlined the plan for Dooley's capture. "He killed Prissie, and he'd kill you, too, without blinking. He knows you ain't Nancy. He got hold of Prissie's mail and there was a letter in it from Nancy saying she was coming to town next week. She wrote it the day you was at the Pantheon, so he knows you ain't her."

"Good, then it should be easy to convince him I am Miss Trevelyn."

Once this was understood, Sally entered into the plan with enthusiasm. "I could say I got a look in your reticule when you was out of the room, and there was a letter in it addressed to Miss Trevelyn."

"Yes, that's a good idea."

"How do you know he killed Prissie?" Beaumont asked.

"When he was here after you left this morning, he had Prissie's watch, that Sir John gave her. A pretty little hunter's watch it was. She never took it off, she was that proud of it. It was real gold, not pinchbeck. She was wearing it when she left London. He must of laid his own watch on the shelf. He pulled out his watch to see the time, and it was hers. He pushed it back into his pocket fast, but I saw it. I let on I hadn't, or he'd have killed me. She never would have given it to him. He killed her. I know it in my bones."

"Have you any idea where we could reach him?" Beaumont asked.

"He never gives no address. I fancy he's looking for you two. He'll be back here sooner or later."

"When he comes, I want you to give him a letter from me. I'll write it now," Lydia said, and asked Sally for a piece of paper.

She discussed with Beaumont what to write. "I'll be the one to meet him," he said.

"No, he might suspect a trick," Lydia objected.

"He knows we are friends. A lady would never go alone on an errand of this sort. It will look natural for you to send your beau. Let me go."

After a moment's pause, she said, "We'll go together."

"Very well," he agreed, although he didn't intend to let Lydia expose herself to such danger.

"What time should I suggest?" she asked.

"We have to go back to St. John's Wood. Make it early tomorrow morning. Just at daybreak. It would be too easy for him to arrange a nasty surprise at night. With his criminal connections, he could have a dozen villains lying in wait for us."

"Why not meet him where he can't arrange any surprises? I mean at Grosvenor Square."

"I doubt he would go there. He'd suspect a trap. Besides, we don't want to involve Sir John."

"Some public place, then," she said.

"Why not here?" Sally suggested.

After some more hurried discussion, Lydia wrote:

Mr. Dooley:

I have what you want. The price is two thousand pounds. Meet me at Prissie's flat tomorrow morning at six. Bring the money if you want the items.

Nancy Shepherd

Beaumont read it over her shoulder. "That should smoke him out. I wonder if he can raise two thousand pounds on such short notice."

"That won't stop him," Sally said. "He'll come planning to knock you out and steal them."

"When he asks where you got the letter," Lydia said to Sally, "tell him I gave it to you. I am sorry to have pulled such a stunt on you, Sally, but I had to do something to find out who killed Prissie."

"All for a good cause. You made a dandy bit o' muslin, miss." Lydia accepted this compliment with equanimity; Beaumont's lips twitched. "Truth to tell, I did have my doubts about you, for you talked so funny, but Nancy was acting as a lady's maid, so I thought that accounted for it. Prissie was my friend, too. My best friend. It's nice of you to go to so much bother for her, her being your da's *chère amie* and all. It would put some girls off, like. I'm real glad Richie's found a good home as well. Can I do anything else to help?"

"Yes, you can get a message off to Grosvenor Square by hansom cab as soon as Dooley leaves you," Beaumont said, and handed her a golden coin. "To pay for the delivery. Let us know what he says when he reads the note."

"I will."

They rose to leave. "Where are you going now?" Sally asked.

"To Bow Street," Beau replied. "I want to have a few officers nearby to follow Dooley and catch him with the evidence on him."

"Will they be able to prove he killed Prissie?"

"They'll try. Someone may have seen him following her at Kesterly, and you can tell Bow Street about the watch—no need to say who gave it to her, but just that she treasured it."

"Don't worry that I'll drag Sir John into it. He was a real nice gent. Always treated Priss like a lady, and me, too, any time I met him."

"Dooley will pay, whether we can prove it or not," Beaumont assured her. "They can only hang him once."

"That's true. I'm glad Richie has somewhere to go. He seemed a nice fellow. I wonder what Nancy's really like. It's good to know Dooley will never get hold of her anyhow. I'll see she finds some nice gent."

They left and returned to Grosvenor Square. Lydia was happy that they had the house to themselves. Her papa was still at Whitehall, and Nessie was out visiting. She asked Blake for some sandwiches, as they had missed their luncheon.

"What time should we leave for St. John's Wood?" she asked as she poured the tea.

"If we leave just around twilight, it will be dark when we arrive. I'll call for you after dinner. Around eight-thirty. How will you get away from Nessie?"

"You are taking me to a rout party this evening, sir."

"Lucky me!"

She looked at him questioningly. "Do you mind terribly, Beau, that I've more or less dragged you into all this? It's not really your problem."

172

"Mind? I am delighted," he said, and looked as if he meant it, to judge by his fond smile. "Who else would rescue you when you overestimated your own abilities but your old childhood guardian, who has rescued you from innumerable trees?"

"Overestimated!" she said at once, rising to the bait. Then she saw the amusement lurking in the depths of his dark eyes and laughed at herself.

As soon as they had eaten, he said, "I shall go to Bow Street now and arrange for company at Maddox Street at six A.M. Let us be there by five-thirty. We'll want to scout out the area. It will soon be over, Lydia."

She took his hand. "You've been very helpful, Beau. I couldn't have done it without you. Most gentlemen would have tried to take over and elbow me, a mere girl, aside."

He just looked at her and shook his head. "Don't think I haven't wanted to. You're not easy to elbow."

"I was sure you would try to keep me away from Prissie's flat when Dooley comes. I appreciate that you treat me like a fully rational human being, and not some foolish child who must be protected from reality. That is so degrading."

After this statement, Beau found it impossible to suggest she remain at home during the last stage of Dooley's capture. Was that why she had said it? He tried to read her thoughts, but he could see no sly light, no laughter or mischief in her expression. She looked genuinely pleased with him. It was amazing how much more attractive Lydia was when she wasn't mounting her high horse.

"Men don't act that way because they think women are foolish," he said. "They just want to protect them because they care for them. Indeed it concerns me that you will be in jeopardy tomorrow morning." He looked at her, wondering if he dared say more. There, where he fully expected to see the stern face of objection, he saw a sweet, soft smile.

"I appreciate that, Beau."

"Then you'll let me go alone?"

"I didn't say that! I appreciate that you are concerned, and I am concerned about your safety, too. We'll look after each other. Dooley is a wily customer, from all accounts. I depend on his greed to overcome caution. And in any case, I shall be armed. I brought my pistol to London with me."

"Do you know how to use it?"

"Oh yes. I have made it a point to be as self-sufficient as possible."

He just shook his head. "Of course you have. You make it difficult for a fellow to be a hero."

"Who wants a hero? From what I have read, they are just show-offs who got lucky. I would prefer a gentleman of common sense."

"That lets me out. I must be mad, agreeing to this harebrained scheme. Let us hope we are both lucky."

He picked up the last sandwich and left.

Chapter Seventeen

Nessie rushed home at six o'clock, pink with pleasure. "Such a day! I was visiting Lady Hertford and who should be there but Prinny! He could not have been kinder, my dear. Such marvelous things he said about your papa. We are dining with the Jerseys this evening. You are invited as well, Lydia, if you are free. I told her you might be going out with Beaumont."

"Oh. Yes, Beau has invited me to a rout party."

"That's nice, dear. You can borrow my Hildie to help you dress for the rout, for I shall be finished with her long before you need to prepare. Your papa will be dining out with me. Ask the servants to make you something nice for dinner. And tell Cook I am expecting half a dozen ladies to tea tomorrow afternoon. As Lady Hertford will be joining me, the prince might possibly drop in. We shall want something quite grand."

She dashed upstairs, still babbling about the prince, so very complimentary.

Lydia relayed the messages to the butler and scampered abovestairs to make her own preparations. The note from Sally had come. Dooley had been back to visit her, and she had given him Lydia's note. He seemed angry, but Sally was sure he would show up at six A.M. as directed. Lydia forwarded the note to Beaumont at Manchester Square.

Having the house to herself was a great advantage in Lydia's preparations. She would not have to leave home in a party frock, which would be inconvenient for fishing in the pond for the plates. She would wear her afternoon gown and a pair of stout walking shoes. Her good evening mantle would conceal the frock from Blake's Argus eyes when she was leaving and returning.

Sir John arrived home just in time to make his evening toilette. He stopped at Lydia's room for a word before leaving.

"Are you still angry with me?" he asked, trying to make light of the situation.

His attitude annoyed Lydia. "What will you do, now that Prissie is dead?" she asked.

His first smile faded to resignation. "I shan't take another mistress, if that is what concerns you, my dear. I have learned my lesson. And with my new duties, I shan't have time for that sort of thing. Truth to tell, I am getting a little old for all that carrying on."

"How very French. La Rochefoucauld said something of the sort, did he not? That when age overcomes our vices, we claim the victory for our own."

"Very likely he did. He also said if we had no faults of our own, we would not take so much pleasure in noticing those of others. Don't look too hard for others' faults, Lydia. I am referring not only to mine, but to Beaumont's. No man likes to be forever apologizing and explaining. A carping woman is no pleasure to be with."

"I hope I am not a carper!"

"You have a tendency that way. I hope you can overcome it or you will lose that lad. He is an excellent parti. I trust you have not spoken to your mama about this Prissie business?"

"Certainly not."

"Good. I am trying to convince her to join me here, as I shall be spending virtually all my time in London now."

"She won't come," Lydia said. She knew it as well as she knew anything. "She would be terrified of meeting prime ministers and princes. She would be happier at home." She would go on embroidering her fire screens and chair covers and wall hangings. No wonder her husband sought solace elsewhere.

Sir John must have been excessively hurt and worried to learn of Prissie's death, and there had been no one for him to turn to. Of course not Mama, and not herself either. She had only carped and complained, harping on her papa's offense, and not thinking on how he must feel. She was not as good a daughter as she might have been. This shocking thought sent her mind reeling.

"I'm sorry, Papa," she said.

"For what?"

"For everything. For my carping, and that you and Mama could not—get along."

"We had a few good years. Perhaps that is as much as one can hope for."

"No, we can at least hope for more. Did I congratulate you on your promotion, Papa? I am very happy for you. You deserve it. You have worked hard all these years. I am proud of you."

She felt embarrassed when she saw a tear start in his eye. Had she never complimented him on his work before? If that was true, she had been a horrid daughter, asking him only what he had brought her when he came home and wanted to boast a little of his various successes.

"That means a good deal to me, Lydia. It will be nice to have you in London when you and Beaumont marry," he said in a husky voice, and left.

How to atone for years of neglect? She could at least keep her father's name free of scandal in this business about Prissie and the counterfeit banknotes. She thought, too, that it would be nice to be in London, near her father, sharing in his exciting life. She could not and would not want to replace Nessie, who had devoted her life to Sir John. Lydia didn't want to live vicariously, forsaking any life of her own, but just to share things as a father and daughter. She thought of Beaumont, too.

Since he had taken his seat in the House, he was taking an interest in politics. It would be a worthwhile project to help him in his career, to offer the sort of companionship and support her papa had been lacking. She felt almost a surge of panic to think of him resorting to the muslin company for such companionship, or worse, to some obliging married or widowed lady. She did not really think Beaumont would be satisfied with such simple folks as Sally or Prissie. He would have no trouble finding more interesting company. Nessie's friends had made a great fuss over him that morning.

She continued with these musings as she ate alone in the formal dining room, wishing she had asked for a tray in her room. How often had her papa eaten alone when Nessie was out? Being alone made a good excuse for not changing into an evening gown in any case. At eight o'clock she went abovestairs and examined her pistol to see that it was loaded and in working order. Her papa had bought it for her at her request. He had always been kind in executing any little order for her. Indeed, he had seemed to take pleasure in doing so. And he had never complained about selecting Mama's patterns and woolens at Mr. Wilks's on Regent Street either. She was bedeviled by a hundred past kindnesses, none of which she had properly appreciated, nor even begun to repay.

At ten minutes past eight, she donned her evening mantle and went belowstairs to await Beaumont's arrival. Newly awakened to her former carelessness, she greeted him warmly when he arrived.

"I truly appreciate all this, Beau," she said. "It is very kind of you to go so far out of your way to help me."

"No need to thank me. I've already told you I'm enjoying it very much. Where is everyone?" he asked, looking around the empty saloon.

"They are out for dinner. Did you make the arrangement with Bow Street?"

"Townsend will have a couple of men lurking about Maddox Street at first light tomorrow. Shall we go now?"

They went out into the lingering twilight of a late June evening. A few carriages stopped in front of other houses, carrying guests to and from their evening's entertainment, lent an air of excitement to the street. This could all be a part of her world, if she moved to London.

The shadows were drawing long as they drove out of town toward St. John's Wood.

179

"We should be home well before midnight," Lydia said. "And tomorrow morning, I shall be up and out of the house for the trip to Maddox Street before Papa and Nessie are awake."

"Then it will be back to Trevelyn Hall, eh?" Beau said.

"Yes, for the summer, but in autumn, I shall come to London to be with Papa."

Beaumont gave her a quizzing grin. "Poor Papa! You will keep a sharp eye on him to see he don't stray again."

"I am not his jailer! That's not why I am coming. In any case, he will be too busy for that. I just want to look after him a little. He's been very kind to me, you know, and I never truly appreciated it. I'm afraid I have been a selfish daughter."

"Modesty don't become you, Lydia. Or is that my cue to recite your manifold virtues? You have never given your mama a moment's worry, other than not making a push to nab a husband."

"I think I have given Papa a worry or two, though," she said, still modest. "He has been lonesome, Beau. I seldom even wrote him a letter, except to ask for things."

He studied her a moment, then said, "All right. What has happened to put you in this slough of despond?"

"I have grown up. That's all."

He patted her fingers. "You have my condolences. It's so nice and easy being a child."

When he realized she was fighting back her tears, he looked out the window, pretending not to notice, but he was touched all the same. What could have happened to soften her former stiffness? Very likely Sir John had given her a good Bear Garden

180

jaw. Should he try to comfort her, or would she cut up at him?

"Much farther?" she asked, before he had made up his mind.

He looked at her then and saw she had dried her tears. "Almost there. We shall stop the carriage at the next corner and proceed on foot. Did you wear stout shoes?"

She lifted her skirt, showing him her stout, laced walking shoes and a few inches of dainty ankle.

"Hussy," he chided, and pulled down her skirt. Then he lifted it again for another quick peek, to show her he was joking.

Overhead, the deep blue sky of twilight had darkened to black with a white moon and a scattering of stars to show them their way. When the carriage stopped, they noticed a gig following them.

"You don't suppose that would be Dooley?" she asked in alarm.

The gig turned in at a farm before it reached them, however, and they proceeded on foot.

"I should have brought a rake or some such thing to fish the plates out of the water," Beaumont said, fully expecting ridicule for not having done so.

"I didn't think of it either. We'll find something at the Nevils' place. The pond should be back there," she said, pointing to the area Richard had indicated that afternoon.

"We'll leave the road here and go through the meadow."

He took her hand, and they slipped quietly through the tall grass that caught at their ankles. Lights burned on the bottom story of the Nevils' house, but there was no one outside to observe them. A hundred yards beyond, they saw the gleam of moonlight on water and increased their pace.

A spreading willow tree grew at the pond's edge. Beaumont looked around for something to use to probe the pond. He found a long, forked branch and began to move it along the water's bottom. Seeing what he was about, Lydia found a smaller branch to probe closer to the edge. She removed her mantle to keep the hem from becoming muddied and hung it on a branch of the willow. The ground there was wet. It was soon squelching through her shoes. The hem of her skirt was sodden, but she kept on probing.

The pond's bottom was six inches deep in mud. Looking for the plates felt like stirring a monumental cake. After twenty minutes, they had encircled the whole pond, and still found nothing. Her arms were tired, her feet were cold, she was becoming frustrated, and she felt guilty for putting Beaumont to so much trouble.

"It may not have been the plates Prissie threw in here," she said. "Perhaps it *was* love letters. And in the worst case, you know, at least no one can use the plates. If we don't find them, I mean."

"This little pond will dry up in late summer. Someone will find them. I'm going to take off my boots and sox and wade in. You have a rest, Lydia. You're gasping."

He removed his boots and sox and hung his jacket on the willow tree. She watched a moment as he continued his probing, standing in water to his hips. He must be terribly uncomfortable. Whatever their mental abilities, she had to concede men were physically stronger than women. Her arms ached, but Beau's strong arms kept moving rhythmically,

182

effortlessly. While she rested, she thought about Prissie and those plates.

"She couldn't throw them very far, only being a woman," Richard had said. If Prissie had taken the path from the house, she would have reached the pond just to the left of the willow. Lydia took up a small rock and pitched it into the pond where she thought Lydia would have thrown the plates. Beau looked all around.

"It was only me," she called.

Then she began to probe about the area where her rock had landed, using her forked stick. It did not reach quite far enough. She took off her shoes and stockings, looped her skirt up around the waist ribbon of her gown, and waded in. The bottom of the pond was horrid, all soft and squishy and muddy up to her ankles. She moved the stick about until she felt something firm embedded in the mud.

"What the devil are you doing?" Beau called in a low voice.

"Thinking," she said, touching her head. She tried to lift the hard object using the stick, but it just moved about in the mud. Sure she had found what they were after, she reached in, and felt a square, mushy cardboard box about eight inches long. She picked it up with a triumphant grin. "Amazing what even a mere woman can do when she puts her mind to it!" she exclaimed.

Beau stared at the dripping parcel and began to wade toward her. "But she can't throw worth a damn. The thing was right on the edge." He reached for the sodden parcel.

"Finders, keepers," she said, laughing as they struggled. "I get to open it. And it is not billets-doux.

It's heavy." She leaned back, holding the parcel at arm's length to keep it from him.

Beaumont leaned over her. She lost her footing and went tumbling into the pond, stifling a scream of dismay. In an effort to save herself, she grabbed on to Beaumont, pulling him in on top of her. She felt the cool water engulf her, seeping into her gown and hair; then she noticed other, more disturbing sensations. Beau's taut body was on top of her, his legs caught between hers, while his weight pressed on her in an engrossingly intimate way. As he tried to rise, his hips thrust against hers, sending a shudder of alarm through her whole body. He lost his footing and moved again in that way that nearly drove her mad. The pond's bottom was soft as a feather tick beneath them. As he struggled to rise, his ragged breath in her ear set off electrifying jolts of excitement. Their wet cheeks clung together a moment; then he slowly, almost reluctantly, lifted his head.

She put her arms around his neck to keep her head from being submerged in the water. His arms were suddenly around her waist, crushing her breasts against his masculine strength to lift her up. He looked down at her, and they just stared into each other's eyes for a long, silent moment, as if they had never seen each other before and were looking at some strange phenomenon. Neither of them spoke, but the silence seemed to echo eerily. Such delirious sensations consumed her that she was reluctant to be rescued. She had never felt anything like this before, as if she were on fire within, yet shivering outside.

Beau gave a push and twisted aside to sit up,

pulling Lydia up with him, her arms still around his neck and his arms around her waist. They both dropped their arms and sat side by side, still without speaking. Mud dripped down her face. Her curls hung in sodden clumps around her ears. Her sprigged muslin looked black.

Lord Beaumont now looked every bit as bad as she did herself. They looked like a pair of mud babies. Sometime during the struggle, she had dropped the precious parcel. She suddenly felt a compulsion to laugh.

"How ever shall I explain this sodden gown when I get back to Grosvenor Square?" she said. "Er, by the way, I've lost the parcel."

Beaumont spluttered and brushed the mud from his eyes. He felt an urge to curse, but when he saw Lydia's laughter, his anger dissipated like a snowflake in the sun. "Shall we dive for it?" he asked.

"It should be right here, where we were —" She stopped in embarrassment. "Where I—"

A wicked grin stretched his lips. "Where you dropped it?" he said, and they began to feel around until she found it.

"Just look at us," she said, gazing down at her disarray.

"Only an engagement can save you from utter ruin now, my dear."

It did not immediately leap to her mind how an engagement could explain her condition, but she didn't say so. The way he was looking at her with that wary, tentative smile suggested it was merely a pretext. "You're right, but I promise I shall jilt you very soon, Beau," she said.

As he reached toward her, her heart began to flutter uncertainly and her breath came in short, panting gasps. His fingers touched the parcel, but instead of taking it from her, his arms went around her, pulling her against him. Below the cold wetness of his shirt, she felt his body's warmth seeping into her. His head hung suspended above hers. His eyes glittered in his muddied face, with a lock of hair dripping over his forehead. She thought he looked marvelously handsome.

"It is the custom for an engaged couple to seal the bargain with a kiss," he said, watching her for signs of either objection or amusement.

She blinked at him, with a fond, foolish smile that encouraged him to kiss her. As her arms went around his neck, he heard the splash of the parcel returning to the pond. Then their lips touched, and they both forgot all about the plates as the first brush of their lips deepened to passion.

"How soon will you jilt me?" he murmured later, with his lips nibbling against her ear.

A soft croon came from her throat. "Mmmm. A month?"

He kissed her again. "Make it a year."

A girlish giggle echoed from below his chin. "Do you think such a long engagement is . . . safe?"

"Who wants to be safe?" His fingers gently wiped the mud from her cheeks. "Make it ten years."

"You are catching cold, Beau. Let us go."

She tried to rise. He pulled her back. "Never! If you jilt me, I shall sue you for breach of promise."

"If you take a mistress, I shall divorce you."

"You will be my mistress and my wife. Sway for me, darling." He drew her into his arms. The water lapped gently around them from their swaying motions.

Wrapped up in their own world, neither of them noticed the two men behind the willow, waiting for them to emerge with the plates.

Chapter Eighteen

Beaumont led Lydia out of the pond, his arm around her waist, their hips bumping familiarly. She was still carrying the plates she had rescued.

"All this trouble, and I don't even know what counterfeiting plates look like," she said.

"Let us have a look."

The soggy cardboard was easy to pull away. She looked at two pieces of wood-backed metal whose engraving was impossible to see clearly in the dim moonlight. She handed one to Beau and examined the other herself.

"All this trouble—Prissie's death and everything—for these stupid plates," she said, shaking her head.

"And for the money they will print."

When Dooley was certain they had the plates, he stepped out from behind the willow, pointing a pistol at Lydia. A smaller man came behind him, pointing his gun at Beaumont.

"I'll take those, Miss Trevelyn," Dooley said in a gloating voice.

She stared at him in disbelief. In the darkness of the shadows, his smile looked infinitely menacing. It was easy to believe he had killed Prissie in cold blood. Then she looked at Beau. She had left her pistol in the carriage pocket. She knew Beau had done the same. Her frustration was nearly as great as her fear. Dooley had already killed once for these plates. He would hardly hesitate to kill again.

His smile stiffened to determination. "Hand them over, now," he barked. The trigger on the pistol clicked ominously.

Beau quickly assessed their chance of escaping alive if they refused and said to Lydia, "Give it to him."

It was the smaller man who stepped forward to take the plate with his free hand. He slid it into his pocket, then turned to Beau. "And yours, mister."

"No tricks, or the lady pays," Dooley added.

His pistol was pointed straight at Lydia's heart. Beau had no alternative but to hand over the plate, which went into the man's other pocket.

Dooley allowed himself a swift smile. "Now back into the water, the pair of you," he ordered.

Lydia saw the murderous rage in Beau's eyes, the dilation of his nostrils, and the rigid line of his lips. She was furious herself but not willing to risk her life. Fearing Beau would do something foolish, she reached for his hand. His fingers were bunched into fists. She tugged at his wrist and led him back into the pond. Dooley and his cohort watched until they were well out into the water; then they turned and ran.

Beau immediately splashed out of the water and went after them, water droplets flying from him in his flight. Lydia tried to catch up, but was hampered by her clinging skirts. He had pulled some yards ahead of her when she heard the shot and saw the flash of light. An instant after the bullet flew, Beau fell. Her heart pounded in horror. If they had killed him . . . She ran faster, stumbling and falling and rising again. Another shot rang out, and she was suddenly on the ground. Had she been hit, too? She lay still a moment, waiting for the searing flash of pain. None came.

Then in the darkness, she realized something warm was gripping her ankle. She hadn't been shot; she'd been tripped. Her scream of terror pierced the night air. She had no idea who or what was clinging to her.

"Shhh! It's only me. Best let them go," Beau said in a low voice.

She sat up and looked at him. "Are you all right?" she asked at once. "Did that bullet hit you?"

"No, I thought it wiser to hit the ground, and to stop you from getting yourself shot as well. The better part of valor, et cetera. Are you all right? I didn't hurt you?"

"You scared the wits out of me."

The echo of hoofbeats on the road beyond told them Dooley had escaped. The back door of the Nevils' house opened, and the sound of men talking came to them from the distance. They would have heard the shots and had come out to investigate. Neither Lydia nor Beaumont felt like answering questions. They lay still until they heard the door close again.

When Beau let out an accomplished string of curses to release his temper, she was in no mood to chastise him.

"Pity they got clean away," she said, "but we're unharmed. He might have killed us."

"They've got the plates on them. I'll notify Bow Street as soon as we get back to town."

"They won't have them by then, Beau. Dooley is awake on all suits. He will have hidden them somewhere and run to ground himself. He must have followed us from town."

"He knew your name. It wouldn't be hard to find out where Sir John lives. Odd we didn't notice them following us."

"There was that gig—but Dooley was on horseback. I expect he kept off the road and followed us from the nearby fields. I wonder who the second man was."

"Just reinforcement. Dooley was running the show."

She shivered, and Beau went back to retrieve their outer clothing. Beau threw her mantle over her, and they put on their shoes.

"We'd best get back to town and out of these wet clothes," he said. "Dammit, I should have foreseen the possibility that Dooley would be following us."

"It's water under the bridge. Let us think what we must do now."

They went back to the carriage—cold, shivering, and thoroughly disappointed at the futility of their endeavor. The coachman looked at them in amazement. When Beau questioned him, the man said he hadn't seen Dooley or his henchman, either coming or going. They had obviously seen their rig and avoided it.

The cruelest blow was that they had actually held the plates in their hands. Lydia was supportive, but Beaumont felt he had let her down. A fellow liked to show to best advantage in front of the woman he loved. But with two armed men, and a lady present besides, what could he do? He had nearly gotten them shot as it was with his foolish attempt at heroism. What would they have done to Lydia if he had gotten himself killed?

191

"I can't take you home looking like this," he said. "You'll have to come to Manchester Square to get cleaned and dried."

"Does your mama have an old gown I could borrow?"

"We'll find something."

The return trip seemed endless. Nothing of an intimate nature passed between them. They were too cold and uncomfortable and dejected. Beau sat thinking how he could catch Dooley, and Lydia wondered just how serious Beau had been about their engagement. He had not actually asked her to marry him. It had all been done in jest, really. He would not have behaved so intimately with her under normal circumstances, but when two people were dumped into a pond together, the normal rules of polite conduct no longer seemed to apply.

When they reached Manchester Square, they still had the ignominy of entering Beaumont's polite mansion looking like a pair of drowned rats.

"We had a dunking in the Serpentine," Beau said to his butler in a voice that did not invite comment. "Lost a bet. Show Miss Trevelyn to a guest room. Find her some dry clothing, and send up a servant and hot water. My valet will take care of me."

Lydia was ushered into a charming guest room done in shades of green and gold. The fire was lit, a tub of hot water was brought, and the cleaning process began. Even her hair had to be washed. The maid was too discreet to ask questions, but Lydia could see her curiosity was on the boil.

"I hope you weren't hurt, miss" was as forthright as the girl dared to be.

"No, not at all. It was a foolish bet."

"His lordship hasn't gone in for pranks like this for years. It's just like old times."

The maid toweled Lydia's hair dry, but it was still too damp to arrange properly. She pulled it back in a knob to keep the wet hair from her neck and gown. As Lady Beaumont was a large dame, Lydia had to settle for a chambermaid's dress, and felt she made a very poor showing in a plain dimity frock when the job was done. She hated to appear in front of Beaumont looking so unattractive, especially when he had changed into evening clothes and looked particularly handsome in a burgundy jacket and gray pantaloons.

His smile was hardly more than formal as he handed her a glass of wine and led her to the grate.

"That's better," he said, looking at her unusual toilette.

"I feel I should be carrying a broom or duster."

"I should be wearing a cap and bells. I feel a perfect fool. How could I let Dooley walk away with the plates? I should have kept after him."

"And gotten yourself killed? Now that would have been foolish. We have already plucked this crow."

"Sane and sensible, as ever," he said.

That was as close to a compliment as he came, if it was a compliment. "You'll want to get straight down to Bow Street. You can drop me off at Grosvenor Square on your way." She took a sip of the wine and set the glass aside. "I'm sorry I put you to so much trouble, Beau."

"I'm sorry I let you down."

"You didn't."

"Just what you expected of me, eh?" he said ruefully.

"We made a mistake. Let us not beat ourselves

over the head about it," she said brusquely. How many times was he going to raise this unpleasant subject?

Beau noticed her scowl and felt worse than ever. "I'll take you home now," he said, equally brusquely.

He put the mantle over her shoulders and they went out to the carriage for the short drive to Grosvenor Square.

"We'll both put our minds to the problem tonight and talk about it in the morning," Lydia said as they drove up to her front door. Beau had not tried to put his arm around her, nor done anything to suggest he loved her. "Bow Street might have an idea," she said.

He accompanied her to the door. When Blake tried to take her mantle, she brushed him away, but she noticed he was looking at her damp hair in a curious way.

With the butler observing them, Beau said only, "I'll call on you tomorrow morning. Sleep tight."

Lydia went straight upstairs, to avoid the butler's curiosity. She thought over the situation as she prepared for bed, and she hid the maid's clothing in her bandbox. Even if they never caught Dooley, this trip had done her some good. She had been jolted out of her complacency. Her knowledge of life had gone from reading books to living—and she had fallen in love. She wondered how she could ever have been so childish as to think she would be happy as a spinster, ignoring all the wonderful fulfillment of love and husband and children.

But did Beau really love her, or had the exuberance of finding the plates led him into saying more than he ought? His silent brooding during the drive home suggested he was unhappy with the situation.

Her strenuous evening left her ravenously hungry,

which made sleep difficult. At midnight she slipped down the back stairs to the kitchen. As it was empty, she made a cup of cocoa and helped herself to bread and butter from the larder. She took a tray to her room and enjoyed the snack. Within an hour she was asleep.

In the morning, she rose early and asked Hildie to help her dress. She had decided that she would make a pitch for Beau, and this called for a special toilette. The blue-sprigged muslin looked well with her black hair, which glistened from last night's washing. Hildie arranged her coiffure in a more intricate do than she usually wore, with her hair drawn up off her face and caught with a blue ribbon in a bundle of curls behind.

She tapped at Nessie's door and poked her head in to say good morning. Nessie took her breakfast in bed. She sat propped up on a pile of pillows, jotting down a list.

"Good morning, Lydia. Did you have a good time at the rout?"

"Yes, a lovely time. How was your party?"

"Wonderful! A wonderful party. I am just making up a list for Sir John's soiree. I must have some sort of do in celebration. You and Beaumont will stay for it, I hope. It will be early next week."

"I'll ask Beau," she replied, and made her escape before Nessie enquired whether she was engaged yet.

Sir John was just leaving for the House when she reached the breakfast room at nine o'clock.

"I have had a letter from your mama," he said, handing her the short note.

"Is she coming?" Lydia asked eagerly.

"Alas, no. Her rheumatism is at her. Pity. I shall try to get home next weekend."

195

Lydia glanced at the note. It was just what she expected. As Sir John would be so extremely busy, it did not seem worth her while to come. Nessie would see to the house, and as her rheumatism was acting up, Lady Trevelyn thought it best to stay at Trevelyn Hall. Perhaps John would pick up some red embroidery wools for her at Mr. Wilks's when he had a moment. Lydia could bring them home with her.

Lydia sighed and set the letter aside. "I'll get the embroidery wools, Papa. You are too busy."

It was just as well Mama was not coming. She would only be an added burden on Papa if she did come. Lydia was sorry, but with her new maturity and compassion, she did not lay blame. It had been an ill-advised marriage. Her mother was a deep-dyed provincial who was unhappy in high company. She should have married some country squire.

Lydia was having her second cup of coffee when Beaumont was announced. Her heart leapt when she saw his beaming smile. He does love me! she thought, and her eyes glowed with delight.

"You'll never credit it," he said, sitting down beside her and giving her fingers a squeeze, when she hoped he would at least buss her cheek. "They've caught Dooley."

"Already! How did they do it?" She was thrilled at the news, but a corner of her mind took note that his smile was not due to seeing her, but to his message.

"A pair of Bow Street officers were in that gig we saw near the Nevils' place. They were following you, to see no harm came to the new Cabinet Minister's daughter. They even saw Dooley hold us up."

"I wonder they didn't come to our aid!"

"They didn't want your name involved at all. They just watched until we were sent back into the pond, then ran to their gig to follow Dooley and his friend, Sanders. Dooley led them straight to the printing shop where the counterfeit money has been made all along. They caught the whole gang. A fellow called Wilkie is in charge. Quite a coup for Bow Street."

"And Papa's name will not be mentioned?"

"Why should it? He had nothing to do with it."

"Oh, I am glad. It helps to make up for . . . everything," she said comprehensively, thinking of her years of neglect and her high-handedness over Prissie. "Will they press charges against Dooley for Prissie's murder?"

"They are looking into it. No doubt someone will have seen him in Kesterly, and there is Sally's evidence of the watch."

"Her being found in Pontneuf River rather points to Papa," she said, frowning.

"Or to me. Or to Horace Findley, for that matter. I doubt she intended to pester Sir John at home. My own feeling is that she wanted a look at Findley's place while she was in the neighborhood, to see where Richie would be raised. She could have learned from Sir John, or at the inn, of the shortcut through the Chase to Findley's estate. Dooley feared she was running to Sir John for help and killed her. No reason any of that need come out at the trial, however. She was running away from Dooley and happened to be caught there. I expect they'll get their conviction. When do you want to go home?" he asked.

The situation went from bad to worse. Now he was eager to be rid of her. And he hadn't even noticed her new coiffure.

"I thought I would stay a few days. Nessie is

having a party for Papa early next week. You are invited, of course. Are you in a hurry to get home?" She peered at him anxiously, noting his frown.

"I am, rather, but I have a few things to do here first. Is Sir John at home?"

"He's left for work."

"Pity. I wanted to speak to him." He sat frowning for a moment, then looked up. "Or Nessie would do."

"What is it you want? Perhaps I could—"

Beau reached out and took her hand. His smile was tender, with love glowing in his dark eyes. "I know you are a very independent lady, but for propriety's sake, I think I ought to speak to your papa, or your chaperon at least. As it is merely a formality, however . . ."

As his fingers closed over hers, a realization dawned. He wanted to ask Papa for her hand. He did love her! Her lips trembled into a smile.

"Are you sure, Beau?" she asked. "If it is only because of last night—because of what you said—"

"My sweet idiot, it is because I have loved you forever," he said, and drawing her to her feet, he kissed her soundly.

Want to know a secret?
It's sexy, informative, fun, and FREE!!!

❧ PILLOW TALK ❧

Join Pillow Talk and get advance information and sneak peeks at the best in romance coming from Ballantine. All you have to do is fill out the information below!

♥ My top five favorite authors are: _____

_____

_____

_____

_____

♥ Number of books I buy per month: ❏ 0-2 ❏ 3-5 ❏ 6 or more

♥ Preference: ❏ Regency Romance ❏ Historical Romance
❏ Contemporary Romance ❏ Other

♥ I read books by new authors: ❏ frequently ❏ sometimes ❏ rarely

Please print clearly:
Name _____

Address _____

City/State/Zip _____

Don't forget to visit us at
www.randomhouse.com/BB/loveletters

regency

NOW IN PAPERBACK

The *New York Times* hardcover bestseller

THE SAVAGE HEART
by Diana Palmer
Author of *The Long, Tall Texan* series

"A wonderful tale of belief and truth that will
wend its way onto your shelf of keepers."
—*CompuServe Romance Forum*

"A riveting, emotional story with an exceptional
couple that readers will remember forever.
Everything about this book is wonderful, making
it impossible to put down."
—*Rendezvous*

In Chicago, 1905, a handsome maverick detective
and a headstrong, rebellious young woman struggle
against their passionate attraction as they try to
untangle a mysterious web of events. Noted for the
sizzle, snap, and soul-stirring emotion of her novels,
award-winning author Diana Palmer will captivate
you with this thrilling romance.

On sale now

NOW IN PAPERBACK

The *New York Times* hardcover bestseller

SOMEONE LIKE YOU
by Elaine Coffman

"An emotionally satiating work that is
an instant keeper . . ."
—*Affaire de Coeur*

"An intensely moving tale of emotional growth
and discovery. Once again, Mrs. Coffman spins
a complex tapestry of the human heart,
a vivid portrayal of life and
the grace and redemption of love."
—*Romantic Times*

In this stirring romance set in nineteeth-century
Texas, a mystery man who appears to be a down-on-
his-luck cowboy and a beautiful young "spinster" hiding a secret past of her own dare to reach for love.
Hailed for the richness and complexity of her work,
Elaine Coffman demonstrates yet again why she is one
of the most beloved romance writers.

On sale now